'I'd rather just stay here.'

Hugh looked at her and spoke with a light caress in his tone. 'Can we knock up some pasta?'

Juliet laughed. 'Inviting yourself to a meal that isn't even made! It's lucky we're old friends, Hugh Beckhill!'

'Old friends?' he drawled softly. 'Are we? I like that idea, somehow.'

Dear Reader

Babies loom large this month! Lilian Darcy takes us to the Barossa Valley vineyards in Australia and an obstetric practice, while Margaret Holt's second book takes us back to the midwifery unit at Beltonshaw Hospital. Two aspects of general practice are dealt with by Laura MacDonald and Janet Ferguson, though single doctor practices must be rare now! Hope you like them. . .

The Editor

Lilian Darcy is Australian, but on her marriage made her home in America. She writes for theatre, film and television, as well as romantic fiction, and she likes winter sports, music, travel and the study of languages. Hospital volunteer work and friends in the medical profession provide the research background for her novels; she enjoys being able to create realistic modern stories, believable characters, and a romance that will stand the test of time.

Recent titles by the same author:

CLOSER TO A STRANGER
THE CHALLENGE OF DR BLAKE

THE BECKHILL TRADITION

BY

LILIAN DARCY

MILLS & BOON LIMITED
ETON HOUSE   18–24 PARADISE ROAD
RICHMOND   SURREY   TW9 1SR

*First published in Great Britain 1992
by Mills & Boon Limited*

© Lilian Darcy 1992

*Australian copyright 1992
Philippine copyright 1992
This edition 1992*

ISBN 0 263 77844 4

*Set in 10 on 11½ pt Linotron Times
03-9209-56257*

*Typeset in Great Britain by Centracet, Cambridge
Made and printed in Great Britain*

CHAPTER ONE

'WELL. . .' Dr Vern Gordon looked significantly at his somewhat younger partner, Dr Geoffrey Steinbeck, and the latter gave an almost imperceptible nod. 'The job is yours if you want it.'

'Just like that?' Juliet Rohan's voice rose musically on the questioning intonation.

'Just like that,' confirmed Dr Gordon. 'Your paper qualifications were so good. . .' He glanced down and paraphrased some details from the computer-printed application that Juliet had worked so carefully over. 'Trained at Royal South Australia, three years' midwifery at Princess Alexandra, the past two and a half years in community nursing down at West Torrens, where, as you've told us, a high percentage of your home visits involved expectant mothers with various problems. The interview was just a formality, really, to make sure you appealed to us face to face.'

'And we're happy to say that you do,' his partner put in.

'I'm glad,' Juliet smiled.

'Frankly, though,' Geoffrey Steinbeck went on, 'this is a bit of a detour from your career path, isn't it?'

'It does look that way,' admitted Juliet, hoping that her answer wouldn't detract from the good impression she had obviously made. 'My career path was starting to seem like a career groove—something I could get miserably stuck in if I wasn't careful, going for promotions and advancements without questioning whether I really wanted them. I wanted a chance to reassess. This isn't a whim, though,' she added hastily. 'I'd love to accept the job and I won't leave you in the lurch by moving on in a few months' time.'

'That was our one concern,' Dr Gordon nodded.

There was a small silence in which Juliet had time to extend her first impressions of the two men. Dr Gordon was in his late fifties, with the fatherly air that seemed to emanate from most obstetricians. His shoulders were comfortably rounded and his middle comfortably soft. Dr Steinbeck was of a sparer build, with thick black hair closely curled on his rather squared head. The square black frames of his glasses completed what might have been a forbiddingly angular set of features if it hadn't been for the wide, boyish smile that frequently pleated each side of his face into deep creases like two sets of brackets.

Juliet sensed—and her senses were usually pretty reliable about people after more than eight years of nursing—that she would get on with the two doctors very well. But what was Dr Steinbeck saying?

'. . .isn't here at the moment, unfortunately.' Damn! She had missed the name. Her attention had wandered at just the wrong moment. 'He's our new partner. We needed to take on a third person to fill all this space.' He gestured expansively.

The office in which they were grouped was large, with high, moulded ceilings. Juliet had not yet been given a tour of the whole place but it did look spacious and pleasant from what she had gleaned from the exterior and the front hallway. Originally a private house, the old single-storey building, constructed in Australian colonial style with a wide veranda on three sides, had been extended at the back and stylishly renovated. There was attractive landscaping in the front garden, and the long back yard had been made into a gravelled car park bordered with native Australian shrubs and trees.

'Speaking of the space,' Dr Gordon put in, 'that reminds me. We're having an informal opening of the new premises this evening. Drinks at five. Do come if you can. Hugh will be there and you can meet him then, as well as having a good look around before the place is inundated with patients and paraphernalia.'

'Then you're not actually using these rooms yet?'

'No, we're still at the old place two blocks away, but it seemed sensible to conduct the interviews here. We move the week after next, Hugh starts the week after that, and yourself a week later still.'

'Would you like to see our set-up now, or. . .?'

Juliet looked at her watch and was slightly horrified at the time. 'I can't, I'm afraid,' she blurted hastily, 'although I'd love to come for drinks and see it then. I'm due to meet an estate agent in Greenough in fifteen minutes. He's showing me a house for rent.'

Dr Gordon laughed. 'You were as confident as we were, then, about yourself and the job!'

'Perhaps,' she answered, and rose, smiling carefully.

Confident? Yes, but desperate, too. Desperate for a complete change of scene after Matthew Evans had got the promotion at the West Torrens health centre that she herself had wanted so badly three months ago. She wouldn't have minded losing the job to him if he hadn't been the type who rubbed it in mercilessly at every opportunity. And perhaps he *wouldn't* have rubbed it in so mercilessly if she hadn't made it politely but definitely clear on several occasions—he wasn't a man who took the hint quickly—that she didn't want to go out with him.

In short, a messy and unpleasant situation. Perhaps, though, it was a blessing in disguise. It wouldn't be the first time in her life that pressure and apparent failure had brought a greater satisfaction in the end.

It's time to leave Adelaide, she thought now as she drove out of Romneyvale and took the gently undulating ten kilometres of road that led to the smaller town of Greenough. And I'm so glad, now, that I didn't get that promotion. I wasn't ready for it, and I might have turned into a Matthew Evans type myself—sneaky and petty as well as ambitious, and losing touch with what nursing is really about.

It was late July in the Barossa Valley. Less than two hours' drive north of Adelaide, the wide, gently sloping valley that curved between low hills was one of Australia's oldest and best-known wine-growing districts, home to dozens of wineries and their adjoining vineyards. At this time of year, there wasn't much evidence of the region's main industry, however. The rough, gnarled branches of the vines, trained so carefully along low wires, looked quite dead, and since it was a Wednesday afternoon there weren't even many tourists taking winery tours or stopping to taste and buy at 'cellar door' sales.

When Juliet swung her small blue car off the road to park it in front of the cottage in Greenough, she saw that the estate agent was already waiting, shifting his feet impatiently on the stone-flagged veranda. His large car sat at an angle on the grass just in front of her own and he had narrowly missed crushing a neglected bed of herbs and flowers beneath one big front wheel. She hadn't warmed to him when she had visited his office first thing this morning, but the tiny bluestone cottage already looked inviting, so she would have to overlook his sharp manner.

Half an hour later she had rented the cottage. It was tiny, with just a single bedroom and bathroom, a small sitting-room in front and at the back an old-fashioned kitchen which was big enough to dine in. At the moment this room was filled with the welcoming glow of winter sunlight, and it was this intimate, welcoming atmosphere that told Juliet at once that this place could be a home.

'Come back to my office and we'll sign the lease straight away,' the young agent suggested, fingering a sharp little ginger moustache.

'All right.' It was only a little after three and she still had two hours to occupy before returning to the new medical building for drinks.

The agent looked satisfied and smug, almost cocky, in fact.

Am I rushing into this? Juliet asked herself, a sudden qualm engulfing her like an unexpected wave in an otherwise calm sea.

Wait a minute, though. . . The job, the cottage. . . Were these the things that were really concerning her? On a sudden impulse, she said to the agent, 'Can I meet you in your office later this afternoon to sign the lease?'

His eyes narrowed sharply, but he drawled, 'Sure! Why not? Need more time to make a final decision, do you?'

'No, it's not that. . .' She suppressed the uncertain note in her voice and added more firmly, since her sudden doubt was none of his business, 'I'd just like to go for a bit of a drive, that's all, and explore the area a little more thoroughly. It's years since I've been to the Barossa Valley.'

'OK, fine,' the man answered, fingering his moustache again as he ushered her back out on to the shaded veranda. 'I'll be in till five. Any time you're ready.'

He had swung his car in a U-turn and roared off, gunning the motor on all cylinders, before Juliet had even started her own engine. As she did so, she glanced in the rear-view mirror and saw that she had accidentally knocked it crooked so that it was now reflecting her own face. A frown creased the creamy skin of her high forehead and her sapphire-blue eyes had papery folds of tension at the corners. To steady herself, she took a brush from her bag and began to pull it through the thick glossy mane of dark auburn hair that framed her face.

That explanation she had given to the man from Dooley Realty hadn't been the whole truth by any means. It was eight years since she had been to the Barossa Valley—nearer nine, actually—and a lot had changed for her in that time. . .

After retracing part of the route to Romneyvale, she took a left turn, drove several miles, and found a smaller road that led up towards the distant hills. Was this the right way? Yes, here it was. . .

She slowed the car until it idled at a standstill and looked at the imposing stone pillars that flanked the gate. Beyond, a tree-lined driveway led to a group of buildings that could only partially be glimpsed, but even from this distance they looked stately and prosperous. The sign above the gate was a new one and even grander than the ones she remembered, but its Gothic lettering was the same: 'Beckhill Wines.' It seemed funny, now, to think of it: eight years ago she had been engaged to marry David Beckhill, the heir to this place and all it produced.

'I wonder where I would be now, what I'd be doing, if David and I had got married. . .'

Unthinkingly, she switched off the engine of the car and sat there, memories filling her suddenly, and images of what might have been as well: a life of luxury, glittering social engagements, fashionable charity work, a light-hearted interest in the business of the winery, and children, of course, to carry on the Beckhill tradition that had begun here nearly a hundred and fifty years ago.

The picture seemed a rosy one at first, but then she remembered what she had been like at seventeen during the year of their courtship and engagement. She remembered her pettiness, her shallowness, the way competitiveness about clothes and men had guided so much of what she did and felt. Some hard lessons had had to be learned at the end of that unreal time, but those lessons had brought changes and satisfactions that she was very glad of now.

'Mrs David Beckhill? No, that's not for me,' she said aloud, and meant it.

Just then, at a silent electronic signal, the big gates of the Beckhill estate opened and a low-slung red Mercedes roared out into the road. Narrowly missing Juliet's small blue Honda as the gates closed again behind, it swerved a little then sped off towards Romneyvale and, presumably, the main road to Adelaide.

Juliet just had time to glimpse a blonde head and the two dark circles of a pair of large sunglasses and she guessed that the woman at the wheel had barely registered the presence of another vehicle. Was that the actual Mrs David Beckhill? She looked about the right age for David. It was a timely reminder that it could be very embarrassing is she was caught by a family member sitting here in the car, and, without regret or reluctance, she started the engine again and drove away.

There were no ghosts of the past to exorcise here in the Barossa Valley, she decided. It would be a wonderful place to live and work, and even a chance meeting with David himself—surely a reasonably unlikely event—could have no power to create pain or regret.

An hour later she had signed the lease on the little bluestone cottage in Greenough and was walking up to the front door of the new obstetrics practice, looking forward to the opportunity of getting to know her future colleagues and work environment.

It was Dr Gordon who greeted her and she saw at once that she was too early. Two women were still arranging plates of hors-d'oeuvres in the large waiting-room at the rear of the building, and Dr Gordon and Dr Steinbeck were obviously absorbed in a professional discussion which it was not her place to join.

'I'll hand you over to Margaret,' Vern Gordon said rather vaguely, leading her towards an older woman who wore a name badge that proclaimed her status as the practice's senior nurse.

'Can I help with anything?' Juliet offered immediately.

But Margaret Chatham took a sympathetic look at the smart cream linen suit and apricot silk blouse that Juliet was wearing and said, 'We're almost finished. Why don't I show you the bathroom and you can freshen up instead?'

'That would be lovely!' She followed the other woman gratefully, realising that it had been a long day—driving up from Adelaide this morning to make sure of being on time, going to the estate agency, lunching lightly on a Cornish pasty and a cup of tea, getting through the job interview, looking at the cottage, signing the lease. . .and that detour to the Beckhill estate. A few moments alone in front of a mirror would be very welcome. Margaret herself looked smart and pretty in a navy skirt, cream blouse and multicoloured hand-knitted cardigan, while Juliet's cream linen probably looked a little tired by this time.

'We have a staff bathroom, but the patients' one is larger, so why don't you use that,' Margaret suggested, 'since we don't have any patients here as yet? Join us when you're ready. People should start rolling up at any moment.'

'Thank you,' Juliet smiled, and Margaret returned the friendliness with a motherly pat on her arm. As she closed the door of the spacious and shiningly new white-tiled bathroom, Juliet put a mental tick beside Margaret Chatham's name—one colleague who didn't seem as if she would create a personality clash in the future.

Ten minutes made all the difference to Juliet's sudden slump in energy. The linen suit was smoothed out and its blouse carefully tucked in, lipstick and meadow-scented perfume were freshly applied and the glossy auburn hair given bounce and shine by another vigorous brushing. Juliet was satisfied with her appearance as she took a last look in the waist-length mirror.

'It won't tell them much about my nursing,' she thought to herself, 'but at least it shows that I try to be pleasant to have around.'

Half a dozen new arrivals were grouped loosely in the waiting-room now, along with the two doctors, Margaret Chatham and the practice's receptionist, Debbie Miller. Not quite knowing who to approach, Juliet made for the food and drinks table and chose a small glass of delicately hued rosé wine but, before she could put it to her lips, Debbie Miller had seized her.

'Dr Steinbeck has deputised me to give you the tour,' she said, setting slight but squared shoulders in the direction of the front hall. 'We'll start with——'

'Miss Rohan!' Now it was Dr Gordon, interrupting

the 'tour' before it had begun. 'I want you to meet our third partner.'

The senior doctor stepped aside a little to present the newcomer at the gathering and Juliet put on the polite, unthinking smile that everyone used when being introduced.

'Hugh,' Dr Gordon said. 'This is Juliet Rohan. Juliet, Dr Hugh Beckhill.'

'Hugh *Beckhill*!' The exclamation came out before she could control it and she felt a flush creep up her neck at once.

But the man opposite her was quite unruffled. 'Juliet! I recognised you across the room as soon as I came in.'

'I take it you two know each other?' Dr Gordon said drily, and, without Juliet quite knowing how it had happened, both he and Debbie had slipped away to join new arrivals, leaving her alone with David Beckhill's cousin.

At least, yes, it *had* to be that Hugh Beckhill. He had recognised her at once, he said, although she could never have said the same to him. He stood there now, smiling at her in a way that managed to contain both confidence and reserve, and for what must have been many long, embarrassing seconds she could only gape at him, repeating his name on a bemused breath. 'Hugh. . .'

Tall, with hair the colour of dark teak prematurely threaded with silver, a calm, confident mouth, hazel eyes. . .

'You didn't recognise me, I take it.'

'N-no.' She could only speak the truth.

'You seem somewhat bowled over by this chance encounter,' he said easily, and finally she managed to draw on a semblance of poise and good manners.

'Yes. I don't know why,' she answered him. 'I

discovered long ago that it really *is* a small world as far as this sort of thing goes. It's just. . .' She took in a breath. Too late to back out now. 'I happened to pass the Beckhill estate today.'

'And it was the first time you'd thought of any of us in years?' he queried lightly.

'Something like that.' She was tingling all over now, and she still wasn't at all sure why. Was it just that she had been thinking of David? Did she mind that his cousin was to be one of her colleagues and employers?

'Come and help me get a drink,' he said. 'And let's talk.'

He took her arm lightly and they threaded their way through the growing crowd in the room. Several people greeted him but he gave only short, bland replies and seemed quite determined that Juliet should remain at his side. At the drinks table he found a newly opened bottle and poured himself half a glass of richly red claret, and Juliet noticed only now that all the wines— grouped at one corner of the table—bore the distinctive Beckhill Estates label.

'So you're our new nurse?'

'Yes, unless you have power of veto?' she quipped, but he answered quite seriously.

'What on earth makes you think I'd exercise it if I did?' The question was accompanied by a sharp glance from his hazel eyes.

'I only meant. . . I was. . .'

'Juliet, are you feeling awkward about this? You seem to be. How long ago is it now since you and David. . .? It must be——'

'Eight years. A little more, actually.'

'And David is happily married. You're surely not

worried that I bear any grudge on his behalf because——'

'I'm not worried about anything. I don't think anything,' she blurted, remembering only as he spoke, about how she and David had hidden the truth of the broken engagement from everyone.

It had been very gentlemanly of him, very much in the Beckhill tradition. After he had told her that their relationship was over he had said it straight away. 'But there's no need to tell people anything. We'll say it was mutual. If you like I'll even. . .well, people can think *you* made the decision if you want it that way.'

'No,' she had said. 'Mutual, if you like. *Not* my decision.' She had been very proud back then, *too* proud, as David had known, to be able to appear before everyone as the jilted fiancée, but a different kind of pride had stopped her from the pretence that she had been the one to do the rejecting.

However, she had not seen David again after the awful afternoon when she had returned his ring—pride again, since etiquette decreed that a jilted fiancée was permitted to keep the ring—and she had lost touch with his circle of friends and family as quickly as if she had emigrated to some distant land.

But it seemed from what Hugh was saying that David had, after all, done as he had suggested and had played the part of the rejected lover. For a moment she was horribly tempted to blurt the truth to Hugh Beckhill but regained her sanity in time. She had to work with this man from now on, and anything involving David was now completely in the past. Any reference to those long-ago events would have to be very carefully thought through.

'Eight years,' Hugh was saying. 'Yes, it *is* that long.

I'm amazed at how little you've changed since the age of seventeen.'

It was the first less than smooth thing he had said, and as she felt herself flush again she noticed that he too looked suddenly uncomfortable.

'That didn't come out right,' he added quickly. 'I didn't mean to imply that you were a giggling school-girl. I wanted to say. . .' He broke off and laughed. 'And I *will* say it. Why not? You were utterly lovely then, and you're as lovely now.' His voice had dropped to a low, vibrant pitch, and the frank compliment was made with a simplicity that Juliet found more disturbing than brash flirting would have been.

'Thank you.' She tried to be as steady in her own reply. Many people had told her she was beautiful. Why should it be disturbing when this man did? 'You seem to be surprised at the fact that I haven't changed.'

'No, surprised to find you here, since you *are* unchanged. I expected you to go into modelling or acting, or to make a marriage as scintillating as your marriage to David would have been, in which case you wouldn't have needed to work at all.' He stopped abruptly. 'But I'm being far too blunt again.'

'You are a little,' she agreed lightly.

Their eyes met for a long moment, and she saw that his pupils were large and dark. 'Sorry,' he said at last.

'Don't apologise,' she answered. 'Instead, let me be just as blunt. You've changed a lot.'

'Yes,' he frowned. 'Perhaps eight years is longer in a man's life than in a woman's.'

'Surely it's a matter of how the time has been spent,' she challenged, and he nodded.

'Perhaps. But that then suggests you've done very little since we last met, and somehow I can tell that's not the case.'

'Well, I think it's a busy span of years in anyone's life,' she began, hoping he would not notice that her light response was evasive.

But he didn't let her get away with it, and brought it straight out into the open instead. 'Look, I'm not probing. Not intending to, anyway. This is a party. We can talk about the weather if you want to.'

The hazel eyes were steady and understanding, and in their depths there was a light of calm humour which he was obviously asking her to share and which she found, in fact, quite infectious. Had his eyes always been like that? If so, why didn't she remember the fact from their meetings eight and a half years ago?

Her memory of him back then was not nearly as clear as it should be. David's cousin. . .hovering on the sidelines at university dances and tennis afternoons and gourmet picnics. Clearer pictures began to fill her mind, and she knew, now, why her memories of him were so hazy. He had been utterly unimportant, then, to the frivolous, spoilt girl she was at seventeen.

She had been interested in the Beckhill heir, not his insignificant cousin. Too thin, too serious and very reserved, completely absorbed in wrestling with his medical studies, pale, bespectacled Hugh Beckhill hadn't possessed the charm and good looks that might have made her notice him in spite of his lesser financial prospects. So he had remained 'David's cousin', the one who tagged along with David sometimes when people persuaded him he needed a break from study.

And now. . .oh, goodness! An even more telling memory was returning. She had presumed that he was in love with her and had treated him with offhand condescension on several occasions. 'Get my bag, Hugh, darling, would you?' 'Oh, Hugh will drive you home, Lisa, if I cajole him for you.' She could only hope desperately that he had forgotten those times.

'You're blushing,' he said, breaking in on her thoughts, and she realised with horror that she hadn't made an answer to his last words. He was right, too. There was a horrible flush creeping up her neck and into her cheeks.

'Hugh,' she said desperately, 'could you show me over the place?'

'Now? Of course!' Then he studied her more closely. 'You'd like to get away from this crowd?'

'Yes, please.'

'No problem.'

Once again he piloted her through the room, only this time they ended up in the wide hall with its moulded plaster ceilings and oak-framed doors. He opened one of the doors and stood back for her to enter. 'Welcome to my office. . . Should I close the door?'

'Yes, please. . . It's very nice, Hugh.'

'Yes, we're all pleased with the set-up here.'

The room was actually more than an office. Two partitioned cubicles that could also be reached through another door served as his examining-rooms, and charts and models in the main part of the room showed that this was where he talked to patients about any problems and questions they had. The beautifully renovated details of the old house provided a reassuring backdrop to the latest in equipment and technology.

'I specialise in infertility,' he said, 'which always seems to make people think of *in vitro* fertilisation these days. Of course a non-urban practice like this one doesn't deal with that, but there's a lot of less complex stuff we *can* do for couples with fertility problems. . .and of course I deal with a lot of very normal and uneventful pregnancies as well. Dr Gordon does quite a bit of——'

'Hugh!' Juliet broke in desperately. Now that they were alone she realised she couldn't get away with this level of light professional chat. 'I have to. . . I want to. . .' She stopped.

She looked up at him—she had been staring at the brand-new pen-tray on his desk—and found that he was quite close to her, studying her with a concerned frown. 'Why don't we sit down?' he suggested gently.

She laughed shakily. 'No, then I'll feel like a patient with a problem. Standing is fine.' They were both just in front of his dark wooden desk, facing each other. She took a deep breath. 'It's simple, really. I want to tell you about what happened eight years ago. I wasn't going to, but I've realised that neither of us will be comfortable working together unless I do.'

'I'm listening, then,' he repeated simply.

'It was David who broke the engagement. Do you remember what my father did?'

'I don't think I ever knew,' he answered quietly, and if he was thrown by her apparent *non sequitur* he didn't show it. 'I assumed it was something of a money-spinning nature. You were obviously very well-off.'

'*Were* being the operative word,' she returned. 'My father was a self-made man. He had a building supply company, quite large, but he made some mistakes, went into a contract that was too big for him, and the company he was supplying went bust. He almost went bust with them, tried to get out of it with some semi-shady dealings and *did* go bust. And it was only a few weeks after that when his light plane crashed north of Port Augusta and he was killed. Don't say anything sympathetic,' she added quickly, then went on, 'My mother and I were left with nothing—nothing, that is, except the fear that my father's death was the result of a deliberate action on his part, and I'm afraid that's something that can never be fully resolved. Since our social position in Adelaide was completely based on my mother's charity work and on her very lavish parties, and since she couldn't afford either of those things any more, the Rohan family fell from favour rather suddenly.'

'You sound bitter about it.'

She managed a smile. 'No. Good guess, but wrong. I'm cynical and very ashamed of how shallow I was then, that's all. There was a time when I minded more about our loss of position than about my father's death, and I can never quite forgive that in myself.'

'I can't believe that's what you really felt.'

'I sorted out my priorities fairly quickly,' she acknowledged. 'David's ending our engagement made the final break between the old life and the new one.'

Images filled her mind as she spoke. It wasn't quite as clear-cut as she was making it seem to Hugh. Those last months at school had been a nightmare. The snobbish clique of girls who had looked on her as their leader had dropped her like a hot coal as soon as her changed status and broken engagement were known. Her sudden iron determination to make something of herself and to pay some kind of tribute to her father's memory by studying medicine had been received with regretful sympathy by the headmistress.

'I'm afraid you just haven't got time to catch up with the work,' Mrs Packham had said. 'I know you're very bright, but you've coasted along for the last four and a half years, doing almost no work at all. Weren't you in the lowest three in your class last year?'

'Yes, but I——' She'd stopped. Impossible to give the reason she had almost blurted out. She had been

madly in love with David—and with his lifestyle—and
school had passed in a haze of tedious classes enlivened
by gossip sessions whenever there was a moment.

'A few months' burst of hard work now, no matter
how dedicated,' Mrs Packham had continued, 'isn't
going to be enough. If you came back next year and
repeated. . .'

But financially that hadn't been possible. Working
harder than she had ever dreamed she would, Juliet
had managed to scrape into the nursing programme at
Adelaide's best teaching hospital, in the last year
before nursing became a college-based training programme. In December, only six months after her
father's death, her mother had married again and
moved to Perth. The man was wealthy but much older,
boorish and bullying. Too proud to ask for financial
help from a man Mrs Rohan had married very frankly
for his money, Juliet went on with her plans to become
a nurse with a very different and far better set of values
than she had had a year before.

But what was Hugh Beckhill saying? 'So you're
telling me that David broke the engagement because
you had fallen from social grace?' His eyes had narrowed a little and she heard a cooler note in his tone.
Obviously he was ready to leap to his cousin's defence.
She had to be honest, though.

'Yes,' she answered clearly. 'I'm not saying it was a
cruel, shallow action on his part. His parents brought
pressure, and——'

'Yes,' he drawled thoughtfully. 'They would have
done. And if I remember rightly——' He broke off
and shot a sharp, assessing glance at her.

'Go on.'

'No, it's. . .'

'You were going to say that Lloyd and Barbara

Beckhill weren't happy about the engagement in the first place.'

'They thought you were both too young. Don't think they spread that opinion far and wide, though,' he added. 'Uncle Lloyd and my father are quite close. I tend to know what's going on in the senior branch of the Beckhill family.'

'It wasn't just the Beckhills, though. My father's death threw me into a state of questioning and change that very quickly meant I wasn't the same person that David thought he knew and loved. I think. . .well, it's certainly a good thing that the marriage never took place.'

She spoke, perhaps, almost too firmly. Hugh turned from her and roamed the room thoughtfully, his paces measured and slow, but if he thought that she was protesting too much he didn't say so. She was very aware of him in the room, and of the silence that had fallen between them now. There was little of his personality in the new office as yet, since he would not occupy it for another two weeks—no family photos, no jacket hung on that antique wooden coatstand.

The empty pen-tray was the most personal object in the room. Made of silver and dark green marble, it was obviously expensive and not simply part of the routine furnishings of a new office. Then a band of engraved copperplate on the pen-tray's surface caught her eye: 'H. C. B. Love always, A. F. B.' Not her business to wonder what those initials stood for or how the name was significant in his life, but it wasn't a gift from a casual friend or a grateful patient, clearly.

But Hugh was speaking again now, standing behind his desk and leaning on it, with his strong fingers splayed. It was quite a wide desk, but none the less he was only a few feet from her now, the small chandelier

overhead bringing out silver and gold highlights in his
dark brown hair. 'I'm glad you told me all that,' he
said, and shot a sharp assessing glance at her. 'We can
dismiss it now, since so much has changed since then,
but if you hadn't said anything things might have been
awkward. This way, we'll be making a fresh start,
and. . .' his voice dropped, and there was a touch of
throaty caress in his next words '. . .I'm looking forward to it quite a bit.'

'Me too,' Juliet nodded, breathless as a sudden thrill
of awareness overtook her.

What did he mean by flirting with her like this? The
potential for it had been sparkling in the air between
them all along, she realised, but he was almost bringing
it out into the open now, and she found the suddenness
of it very disturbing. An hour ago, she had barely
remembered who he was.

'And I'm glad it's all in the past as far as you're
concerned,' Hugh went on, 'because you'll be running
into someone else who will bring back memories of
that time. I've been seeing Alicia Beckhill for an
infertility problem for the past two years in Adelaide,
and now that I'm moving to this practice she'll be
coming here.'

'Alicia. . .?' The initials on the pen-tray, perhaps.

'Yes,' he nodded smoothly. He was studying her
intently now, and she might only have imagined that
teasing moment of awareness just seconds before.
'Alicia,' he repeated seriously, holding her gaze with
his own. 'David's wife.'

CHAPTER TWO

JULIET carefully squeezed the rubber bulb of the dropper above the HCG reaction disc and several drops of liquid fell accurately. She then went to weigh Mrs Henschke quickly while she waited for the pregnancy test result to appear. The practice was busy this afternoon. Dr Steinbeck had been called to the hospital half an hour ago and Debbie Miller hadn't been able to contact two of his patients who were scheduled for this afternoon, so Hugh was squeezing them on to his list instead, although it was already a full one.

'I know I've gained too much,' Mrs Henschke said as she stepped on to the precisely weighted scales.

'Four and a half kilos, just about,' Juliet replied.

'In four weeks! That's terrible!' the young woman moaned.

'Actually, it's just about perfect,' Juliet said firmly. 'You're in your fifth month and you were so sick up until six weeks ago that you lost several kilos. You need this spurt now, and a similar gain over the next month.'

'Do I? But look at my hips. . .'

'That's not hips, that's baby. Have the diet booklets we gave you been helpful?'

'Oh, yes! I've actually learnt some new recipes that Rob really likes. And all the things that I'm not eating and drinking—like coffee and Cola and chocolate—I'm not missing at all.'

'Then I'd say you're doing fine,' Juliet said, noting down the weight. 'Dr Beckhill is still with another patient, so pop back to the waiting-room and we'll call you in a few minutes.'

'Right-oh,' Jill Henschke said, picking up her bag and walking back through the hallway, her posture and gait still unaffected by the bulge that was growing daily at her waist.

Juliet returned to the small room where urinalysis and other simple routine tests were conducted. Looking at her watch, she noted that the correct amount of time had passed. There should be a result by now. She picked up the neat disc and examined it quickly. Negative.

'Oh, *no!*' she whispered, the disappointment hitting her like a physical blow. Better break the news straight away. She knocked on Hugh's office door and entered at once.

Alicia Fenway Beckhill turned and half rose, her strained face eager at first and then grooved by lines of pain and disappointment as she saw Juliet's grave face.

'Negative,' the latter said briefly. 'I'm sorry.'

She let herself out without waiting to hear what Alicia would say. It was Hugh's place to give comfort and encouragement. Alicia had been so sure, cataloguing symptoms that came straight from a dozen books on pregnancy. 'I've been queasy the past three mornings, and I can't stand the smell of coffee or cigarettes, I feel dizzy, bloated. I'm two days late. I know that's not much but I'm usually so regular. . .' she had bubbled to Juliet fifteen minutes ago.

But it had only been wishful thinking, and the symptoms were caused mostly by the strain of wanting to be pregnant so badly. The lovely blonde was only two years older than Juliet but looked several years older than that.

'I know you from somewhere, don't I?' she had said

when she first arrived today, and it turned out that they had been at school together, although Alicia had been two years ahead.

So this was the woman David had married! Juliet had thought, curious and a little uncomfortable about the whole thing at first, especially when the penny dropped in Alicia's mind. 'Juliet Rohan. The name sounds. . . Oh, of course. You were the girl that——' Her face stiffened visibly.

'Yes,' Juliet had smiled carefully. 'What a long time ago *that* seems! I probably wouldn't know David now if I saw him in the street.'

'And yet you're working for his cousin,' Alicia had frowned, still hostile and suspicious.

'Yes, it's quite a coincidence, isn't it? And I *didn't* recognise Hugh when Dr Gordon introduced us.'

'David hasn't mentioned it. . .'

'I doubt if Dr Beckhill has remembered to tell him. After all, this is only his second week in the new practice, and my first.'

'Well, I must remember to tell him, then. I'm sure he'll be interested to hear where you've washed up.' The comment was a little catty—understandably so, perhaps—in its implication that to be a nurse was to have sunk to low depths indeed, but then the meticulously groomed Mrs Beckhill had patted her stomach in a tentative, hopeful way as she confided her optimistic list of symptoms, and Juliet's place in her husband's past was forgotten—for the moment, at least.

And then, ten minutes later, had come the disappointment of the negative test result. It wasn't easy to be the bearer of those bad tidings. Now, as Juliet did the routine urinalysis of Jill Henschke's specimen, she heard Dr Beckhill's door open and saw Alicia enter the hallway, her face pressed into a linen handkerchief and a strand of her blonde hair dampened by tears.

She went through to the waiting-room without glancing across to where Juliet was, and just before the far door closed behind her unhappy figure Hugh appeared in the doorway, looking after her with a rueful, helpless expression. He caught sight of Juliet and crossed the short distance that separated them to stand leaning against the door frame of the small room.

'We shouldn't schedule people like Alicia in with everyone else,' he said. 'It's too hard on them. No doubt that waiting-room is full of bulging tummies. . .'

'Yes, and Mrs Dempster is here for her six weeks post-partum check, and she's brought baby Lauren.'

'Yes, I heard the little thing crying. Poor Alicia!'

'She seemed so certain about it, too.'

'Not for the first time, Juliet. She talks herself into the symptoms. But I've got patients waiting, haven't I?'

'I'm afraid so.'

'Send Jill Henschke in, then.' He turned on his heel and went into his office, leaving the door open so that she could see him prowling there restlessly as she noted the results—normal and healthy—of Mrs Henschke's urinalysis, and went to call her from the waiting-room.

Then, as she took the twenty-four-year-old's blood-pressure and pulse in the first of the small examining-rooms that adjoined Dr Beckhill's office, she heard him on the phone.

'David? Hi! Hugh, here. Look, I'd like to talk to you privately about. . .'

She heard no more of the conversation as Jill Henschke began to speak. 'I'm starting to get so hot in bed at night. Is that normal?'

'Quite normal,' Juliet smiled. 'Your whole metabolism is chugging along more strongly. You'll probably get hotter by the end.'

'Thank goodness it's due before the worst of summer, then!'

By the time Mrs Henschke finished chatting with Juliet about some of her small, very natural questions and worries, Hugh had ended his conversation and was ready to examine his patient.

More patients came and went in a steady stream for the rest of the afternoon, leaving Juliet with little time to think. Dr Steinbeck returned at half-past three from a safe delivery of twins by Caesarean, so the backlog was cleared and the last patient departed at half-past four. Dr Gordon had left half an hour ago for his Friday afternoon golfing practice and Margaret Chatham was about to take the day's blood-work to the pathology lab in Gawler, while small, energetic Debbie had hurried off to collect her ten-year-old twins from after-school sports.

In short, the place was suddenly very quiet. As she tidied up files and equipment, not yet working as efficiently as she usually did, since this was only her fifth day at the new practice, Juliet had time to wonder what Hugh was doing. He had remained in his office after seeing his last patient, and there was silence behind the closed door.

He was a good doctor to work for. She had concluded this after the first day. He had been well-informed about each patient and did not rush Juliet through the preliminaries that she was responsible for—urinalysis, weight, blood-pressure. He wanted to hear, too, if she had anything special to report, and had already shown signs of trusting her intuition and judgement. He even had legible handwriting!

If she was a little disappointed that those distinct

sparks of awareness between them three weeks ago at the opening of the new building seemed to have dissipated in the cold light of routine working days, she didn't allow herself to dwell on the fact.

She was just debating whether or not to knock on his door simply to say goodbye when she heard his pager go off, and a minute later he emerged from his office at last.

'Juliet! Thank goodness you're still here!' Then he noticed the tailored outdoor jacket of grey wool that she had just taken from the peg behind the door. 'But you're about to go.'

His disappointment was so patent that she hastened to assure him, 'I'm only on my way home. It can wait.'

'I assumed you'd be going out.'

'Not tonight.'

'Then would you mind waiting? You see, I'm expect-ing——' He stopped abruptly, then went on in a different tone. 'No, I won't explain. The quicker I'm gone, the quicker I'll be back. It's Miranda Brown. Contractions five minutes apart and she's on her way to the hospital, but it's a first pregnancy so I should be able to get back here after I've taken a look at her. It could well be hours before I'm needed again.'

'I'll wait, then,' she agreed.

He was already on his way out of the door, shrugging firm shoulders into a jacket of soft brown leather, but he tossed her a last smile of thanks that made her think—and not for the first time this week—that he really was unfairly good-looking these days, with that shock of slightly untidy dark hair, those sensitive, intelligent eyes, that confident bearing. The bevy of girls who had sighed after David Beckhill eight and nine years ago might have done better to take more notice of the serious, intelligent cousin who had been so much in the background back then.

Sitting down to look through the filing system in order to familiarise herself more with what went on in the practice, she wondered whom he was expecting here this evening. A patient? A friend? It was quite possible that she wouldn't find out, since he seemed fairly confident that he would be back here before his visitor arrived.

But at half-past five the phone rang, and she wasn't really surprised to hear Hugh's voice on the other end of the line. Labour was never predictable. 'She's eight centimetres dilated already and going strong. I'll have to stay and see it through. Don't wait, Juliet. I shouldn't have asked you to. Leave a note on the door and——'

'Wait a minute. A car has just pulled in now,' she interrupted, hearing the crunch of tyres on gravel in the car park at the back of the centre. 'I'll just tell. . .' She hesitated then came up with a diplomatic phrasing. 'I'll tell your visitor what has happened and you can arrange something between you.'

'Juliet, perhaps I should have told you——'

'Don't worry about it. I really didn't have anything else to do tonight,' she cut in quickly.

Not that she wanted to be dogsbody to this man or to anyone else, but she didn't have the impression that he was the type to exploit someone else's willingness, so she was not at all put out about this one occasion. That flip through the files had been interesting and useful.

'All right,' he was saying. 'I won't make an issue of it by—— Oh, damn! Never mind! I've got to go. See you later.'

He rang off before she had a chance to say anything

more and she wondered what those last impatient,
irritable phrases had been about. Last night's emergency work on an older patient in premature labour,
probably, more than the current mix-up. In other
words, he was simply tired. He had been looking so all
day after that two a.m. call-out.

She heard footsteps on the slate walk that led to the
entrance and stayed waiting behind the white laminex
reception desk. The footsteps paused just outside and
she knew one moment of vague fear—it was dark
outside, it was a man's tread, and she was alone here—
then the door opened and after a frozen moment of
disbelief and uncertainty she knew why Hugh had
seemed uncomfortable about asking her to wait.

The man who stood there, frowning and not really
looking at her, was David Beckhill.

'Excuse me, I'm here to see Dr Beckhill. Is he
around, could you tell me?'

He doesn't recognise me! was her first shocked
thought. And yet Hugh said I hadn't changed! Then
she realised that in fact David simply had not bothered
to look at the face above the white uniform behind the
desk. To him she was simply that—a uniform behind a
desk, a service person, there in order to answer questions like the one he had just tossed at her in that
polite neutral way.

'No, I'm afraid he was called to the hospital,' she
answered, playing the role. 'He asked me to tell
you——'

'Juliet Rohan! It can't be!' he breathed as his eyes
focused on her face at last.

'But it is,' she answered calmly. So Hugh had said
nothing to Alicia *or* David! Perhaps he had been
planning to mention it to his cousin tonight.

'You're working *here*! As a secretary!'

'A nurse, actually.' Her almond-shaped fingernails touched the dark blue name badge she wore, with its raised lettering that read, 'Sister Juliet Rohan'. Then, briefly, she summarised the situation, making it quite clear to David that they were here together like this through pure coincidence.

As she spoke, impressions were flooding her. So this was David! She had thought him ideally handsome once. Straight black hair, brown eyes, dark neatly curved brows, perfect white teeth, and with an ease of bearing that had seemed to her at seventeen like the confidence of a man who would one day rule an empire—a modest one, of course, but an empire none the less.

Now, immediately and inevitably, she saw all these things differently. To an unthinking gaze he was still as handsome as ever, but she found that her own deeper assessment was a little more critical. The thick hair came too low over his forehead, as if he was subconsciously afraid that his brow lacked strength and shape. His eyes seemed too restless now, reminding her of difficult young interns who were on the look-out for any opportunity to advance their fledgeling careers. They were the eyes, perhaps, of someone too accustomed to being important, and not yet accustomed enough to the hard work that went with it. And his ease and arrogance were surely a little untested, and a little brash. He was still very much an apprentice to his father, and his flair for wine and the winery business was by no means a proven thing.

But perhaps she was being too harsh and unforgiving in her judgement, and it shocked her to discover that this inevitable meeting was rocking her equilibrium so quickly.

'My God!' David breathed again when she had

finished the terse autobiography. 'I assumed. . . I had
no idea you'd even stayed in South Australia.'

'Well, I did,' she returned.

'I felt so bad about everything that happened,' he
went on, seeming not to notice her flip manner,
designed to signal that she had no desire to rehash
what might have been—now, or at any other time. 'So
often I wished I'd bucked the system and refused to
stop seeing you, but back then. . .family pressure. . .
and Alicia waiting in the wings. She wanted a summer
wedding and I told myself that it was the best antidote
to you—to fall as much in love with Alicia as I could
and marry her as soon as possible.'

'I'm glad it worked out so well, then,' she put in,
deliberately misinterpreting his hint that Alicia Fenway
had been very much a second choice. 'And you're
hoping to start a family now. That's marvellous! Speaking of which, you're here to see Hugh, aren't you?'

'Yes, but——'

'I'm afraid he just called from the hospital. A
patient's labour is going much faster than he thought it
would and he won't be able to get back here after all.'

'Juliet, hey, it's me, David Beckhill, remember?' he
cajoled eagerly, his dark eyes warm and boyish suddenly. 'Not John Citizen, future father. We've got a lot
to talk about. Can't we relax?' He came towards her
and reached out a hand, trying to coax her from behind
the reception desk where she stood stiffly, the usually
graceful lines of her figure angular and rigid now.

Before his fingers had firmly made contact with
her bare forearm, she shook them off and met his
gaze squarely. 'David, isn't it best if it's like that?
The relationship we once had is in the past and both
of us want it to remain so,' she said very firmly. 'We
move in different worlds now, and those worlds only

meet here, where Alicia's well-being is the only concern. Treat me as a nurse, and I'll treat you as the husband of a patient and nothing can go wrong. Otherwise——'

'Yes, yes, you're right,' he nodded. Two spots of unexpected colour had appeared on his cheeks, and he stepped back a pace, holding himself in a way that would have had no Beckhill ancestor ashamed of him. He was well-built, still, with no sign of superfluous flesh. 'I'm sorry. Hugh wanted to see me. What was it about, do you know?'

'No, I'm afraid I don't.' She didn't add that Hugh hadn't even told her who his visitor would be.

'Because if it's the same old routine,' David went on in a more aggressive tone, 'tell him the answer is no. We already know which side of the equation the problem is on, so what's the sense in going through any further tests on my side? Tell him that, will you? Exactly that.'

'Of course,' she murmured, a little taken aback by his sudden hostility to the cousin he had been so close to eight years ago.

'If he wants to talk about something else, tell him to drop round to the estate tonight,' David went on, and his tone was warmer again now. 'For dinner if he likes. We've got some American importers over at short notice, and his angle on the business is always appreciated. Only if he's free, of course.'

'All right.' Belatedly, she scribbled the message down on a yellow message pad and wondered whether to try and get hold of Hugh at the hospital through his pager, or ring him at home later instead.

The hostility in the first part of the message seemed a very personal thing, and she wasn't sure that she wanted to get involved in it, even in the neutral role of relay. Unfortunately, David had left her with little choice, and the dinner invitation meant that she couldn't simply leave the message on Hugh's desk for him to encounter next time he came in.

'I'd better be going, then,' David said, as he watched her rapidly moving pen. 'It was—er—nice to run into you again.' His stiff adoption of her own distant manner was almost comical—or would have been if Juliet hadn't felt very uncomfortable, still, about the whole meeting.

'Yes, it was,' she managed to nod, her wide smile not quite reaching her eyes. His smile, too, was somewhat forced, and when he backed towards the door, fumbling in the pocket of an English wool coat for car keys, she knew a great relief that the encounter was almost over.

'No doubt we'll see each other again,' he said finally. 'But in the meantime, best of luck. Bye.'

'Bye.'

The wide wooden door clicked behind him and Juliet was thankfully alone. Checking and locking the building, she wondered about delivering the message, and finally decided to call Hugh's home number, written here on the staff contact sheet pinned to the wall behind the reception desk, as soon as she reached the cottage. She would get his answering-machine, no doubt, but that was probably for the best, and if he arrived home too late to get to the dinner it was probable that he would be too tired to be interested in an evening out anyway.

With the issue satisfactorily resolved, at least on the surface, Juliet left the building, climbed into her small blue car and drove home along the dark, wintry roads.

The cottage was chilly when she let herself inside, but she had laid a fire in the stone hearth this morning, and when she touched a match to twists of newspaper at the bottom of the careful stack of kindling and gum logs a bright orange blaze soon roared into life, filling the cottage with the crack and hiss of steaming resin and the tang of smoky eucalyptus oil.

'Now, that message,' she murmured to herself as soon as her hands were warmed over the flames.

Still in the smart white uniform with its heavy piping at collar, sleeves and hem, she went to the phone and dialled, hearing Hugh's rehearsed tones as she expected after five rings.

'Hello, you have reached Dr Hugh Beckhill. I'm not available at the moment. . .'

Somehow, though, she didn't succeed in speaking after the tone in the calm, fluent way she had run over in her mind, and the words came out at a stumbling pace. 'Hugh, this is Juliet. Er—I. . .well, David asked me to tell you. . . He wanted to know. . . Never mind. Please ring me when you get in.'

She dropped the receiver back in its cradle, cursing her clumsiness. He would think her very inept. That was the worst of answering-machines. You could tear up a letter before it was sent, and awkwardness in conversation left no lasting record, but a message on a machine was stuck there foolishly waiting for its listener. Oh, well, nothing to be done about it now, and really the whole thing was between David and Hugh.

Feeling a little jaded by the day, she went to her room and changed into black wool trousers that tapered at the ankles and tucked into pleats below the fitted waistband, topping them with a soft mohair pullover in a sapphire shade that heightened the colour of her eyes and made her hair seem like the flames of that glorious fire in the next room. Pretty, comfortable, cosy clothes. They made her feel a lot better.

Next, donning a ridiculous apron in a loud pattern of
unlikely blue roses, she went to the kitchen and got out
salad ingredients, cheese and eggs. A cheese omelette
was just the light yet nourishing fare she needed this
evening. Why? Because the unexpected encounter with
David Beckhill had taken that much of a toll on her
sense of peace and well-being? Surely not!

A knock at the door startled her so that the first egg
went splattering into the china mixing-bowl, shell and
all. Instinct told her as she headed for the door who it
would be, and she began to tear at the bow that
fastened her apron at the back. Seizing the wrong end,
she only pulled it tighter, however, and she was able to
fling it desperately aside behind the couch just a second
before opening the door.

'Hello,' said Hugh out of the dark space of the
veranda. There was no outside light.

'Hi! Come in,' she answered nervously, and then it
occurred to her for the first time that he probably
expected her to be angry.

Strangely, though, she wasn't. Rather, she felt a
pleasing warmth inside her that was akin to the glow of
the flames still leaping freshly in the grate.

'I came to apologise for sticking you with that tedious
wait at the end of the day,' Hugh said, stepping inside
and glancing appreciatively at the small lounge-room.
Juliet was pleased that she had worked so hard over
the weekend to make it homey, putting up prints and
pictures, hanging curtains and arranging plump, inviting cushions on the twin couches that had furnished
her rather ordinary flat in Adelaide until last week.

'It was no trouble,' she responded lightly to his
words as she wondered what to offer him to drink.

'Well, no, I should have managed the thing better.

I'm sure it was awkward for you. . . At that hour, and
with——'

'If you mean because it was David. . .' she came in.
They were facing each other, both having instinctively
moved towards the inviting warmth of the fire.

'I'm not suggesting——' he began, but she interrupted evenly again.

'You *do* mean because it was David. Don't be tactful
about it, please, Dr Beckhill. That only suggests that I
still feel something for him, and that isn't the case.'

'Isn't it? Good.' He was studying her intently but
distantly, the dark pupils of his hazel eyes liquid and
unfathomable in the mellow light.

'I get the impression you don't believe me,' she
blurted. He was definitely keeping something back.

'I believe you. I just hope. . .' He stopped.

'Yes?'

'I just hope it's true in David's case as well, that's
all.'

A tense silence fell, and now was not the time to
suggest wine or coffee. His words confirmed the uneasy
feeling she had had about David's reaction to her
reappearance in his life.

'I shouldn't have said that,' Hugh growled. He had
turned to the mantelpiece and laid his hands on it,
blindly studying the simple glazed vase that stood
there, crowded with white and gold daffodils.

'I'm sure it isn't true,' Juliet lied, then, stretching the
truth a little more, 'He didn't recognise me at first
tonight.'

'I can't believe *that*. . .' He turned to her suddenly
and his gaze swept frankly from the luxurious fullness
of her hair to the curves of her figure revealed by the
soft clinging shapes of mohair and wool. He added,

'He probably just didn't notice you because you were in uniform.'

It was so exactly what she had decided herself about David's initial reaction that she almost laughed aloud—Hugh Beckhill certainly knew his cousin well. But his next words quickly cured her of amusement.

'You've got some idea, now, of Alicia's fertility problems. It's not bringing them closer together in their marriage at the moment. We've pinned the problem to Alicia, but I'm becoming convinced that it doesn't end there and I want to run some simple tests on David as well. He won't hear of it, and it's straining relations all round.'

'Should you be telling me this?' Juliet broke in anxiously. What he said was putting several things into perspective, and making sense of David's angry message, which she still had not relayed, but being privy to such a personal problem made her deeply uncomfortable. 'I feel that it's breaking——'

'I'm not telling you as gossip,' he put in impatiently. 'Forget that you were his fiancée once. You said it was all in the past. But Alicia is a patient and professionally it's something you're bound to find out—and something you need to know. David's attitude is a problem.'

'Yes, you're right,' she murmured, frowning. 'It *is* something I should know.'

'But you hate knowing it?'

'Hate is too strong a word, but yes, how could I not feel uncomfortable?'

'Hm.'

'Hugh. . . Dr Beckhill, if——'

'Hugh is fine,' he said. 'Tonight and from now on.'

She nodded quickly and went on. 'If you think it's because I was once engaged to him. . .'

'Juliet, we're going round in circles,' he came in gently. 'Perhaps I should go. Unless. . .'

'Yes?'

'Would you like to eat somewhere? Unless you have other plans.'

'No, I'd love to—— Oh, heavens! I forgot!' She clapped her hand to her mouth.'

'You *do* have other plans?'

'No. David's message. You're invited to dinner at the estate tonight if you want to go. There are some visiting American importers, and you should ring David, too, because. . .well. . .he confirmed what you said earlier. He doesn't want to be tested for a possible fertility problem. He said it rather cryptically, but——'

'But somewhat stronger in wording than what you've just relayed. Damn David!' Hugh clenched his teeth suddenly. 'No, I don't want to go and meet a lot of wine people. I'm not dressed for it, I'm tired, and I'm not in the mood. Actually. . .' He looked at her and spoke with a light caress in his tone. 'I'd rather just stay here. Can we knock up some pasta, or something?'

She laughed. 'Inviting yourself to a meal that isn't even made! It's lucky we're old friends, Hugh Beckhill!'

'Old friends?' he drawled softly. 'Are we? I like that idea, somehow.'

'I do, too.'

The breath caught slightly in her throat as she spoke, then they smiled at each other in the glow of the firelight, with an open acknowledgement that what was starting to happen between them was very nice indeed. For the moment, David Beckhill was quite forgotten.

CHAPTER THREE

'So of course the horse bolted, I landed flat on my. . .
well, you get the picture. And so now one of Australia's
best-known food and wine writers thinks there's a
strong streak of insanity in the Beckhill family.'

Juliet's shoulders shook helplessly and she had to
wipe tears of laughter from her jewel-blue eyes. Hugh's
account of the undergraduate prank, involving a horse,
a dozen eggs and a gaggle of bemused onlookers, had
been given with the flair of a true comedian, and once
again she couldn't believe that this entertaining companion had been the young man she had dismissed as a
stuffy and tedious bore eight years ago.

'And what happened to the eggs?' she asked, when
she could manage to speak at last.

'Oh, they went into the pan.'

'They *did*!'

'Yes, minus a few splashes. Needless to say, though,
it wasn't the omelette of the century.'

'And the horse. . .?'

'Was found ten minutes later happily enjoying the
grass in his home paddock.'

Silence fell between them for the first time since the
meal began. Plates, wine glasses and salad bowl sat
empty in front of them now as they looked at one
another across the small wooden kitchen table, on
which bright appliqué table-mats, white china and tall
red candles in elegant black holders combined to lend
a note of graciousness to the simple meal.

'Would you like some more wine?' Juliet asked. 'It's not Beckhill Estates, but——'

'I can get you a crate if you'd like one.'

'Oh, heavens, I wasn't fishing for a free sample.'

I know, but will you take it all the same?'

'It would be lovely. I like wine, but I'm a very moderate drinker. A dozen bottles will probably last me two years.'

'I'm the same. For business when I have to. For pleasure. . .only when I'm really ready to relax and appreciate the finer things in life.'

He accepted her offer of more wine with a nod but signalled 'enough' when the glass was less than half full. The subtle compliment—that he felt relaxed in her company and that she herself was one of the finer things in life—had brought a tinge of pleasurable pink to her cheeks. To cover the rather alarming fluttery sensation that went with it, she said, 'So you have quite a bit to do with the business of the winery?'

'As little as I can help. Several years ago I spent some time getting to know the business, since I have a parcel of shares in the company, and it means that when something comes up that I have to be involved in I know what I'm doing. Basically, though, I'm very glad that the burden of inheritance will fall on David's shoulders. My calling is medicine, and if there had been something in the way of that, a duty elsewhere, things might have been very hard. As it was, Uncle Lloyd was angry with me for quite a while about my choice of career. Sometimes I think he still is.'

'Mm,' she murmured thoughtfully, staring into the flickering flame of the candle that was burning lower and lower in front of her. 'I'd never thought of it in that way—that inheriting a successful company could be a burden as well as a prize. I wonder if David. . .?'

But it was something she should not have mused about aloud.

'There's no problem for David,' Hugh came in crisply, jerking Juliet's gaze from the hypnotic golden light of the candle. Across the table she could see that his brow was furrowed above those thoughtful hazel eyes. He saw that his reply had startled her and said quickly, 'Sorry. I snapped, and I shouldn't have.'

'Don't apologise.'

'No, I'm getting a little tired, that's all. After we got Helen Lucas's premature labour to stop last night, Susan Jennings was nearly ready to deliver, so I didn't bother to go home, and, by the time that was safely over, I came straight in to the surgery.'

'Hugh! You should have reminded me. I know you said when you came in that you'd safely delivered a frank breech, and I knew Helen Lucas had had some trouble, but I wasn't thinking about what that must have meant to your energy levels.'

'I'm used to it,' he smiled evenly. 'Don't worry. This fatigue has only just hit. Although if those Radcliff twins decide to appear later tonight I'll probably consider switching to dermatology.'

'Dermatology?'

'Yes. The hours are nine to five, Monday to Friday. I mull over the idea several times a month, and somehow it's always at three in the morning on the way to the hospital!'

She laughed and forgot about the short moment of ill humour he had betrayed. 'The Radcliff twins aren't due for another three weeks or more,' she reminded him.

'They'll be here before that. When I examined Mrs Radcliff two days ago she was already effacing, was two centimetres dilated and she'd had some Braxton

Hicks contractions that had kept her awake for three hours on Tuesday night.'

'Perhaps you should go home and get some rest.'

'No "perhaps" about it. I should have left half an hour ago, but this has been so delightful, Juliet. . .' His voice had taken on that caressing note that made her spine tingle as strongly as if his hands had been there warming her flesh with tender strokes.

'Yes, it has, hasn't it?' she agreed, glad that he had risen so that she could do the same and turn from him to conceal the hot tide of awareness that had coloured her cheeks.

She picked up their empty plates to carry them to the sink, but before she could move away from the table his arms had wrapped around her and she felt his warm breath whispering through her hair. 'Put those down,' he growled.

'Hugh. . .'

'Juliet. . . Isn't this what you want? I know I do.'

He turned her to him and touched his lips to her forehead then lifted her chin with his hands and found her mouth, parting her lips with teasing rhythms. The fresh, golden taste of the wine still lingered on his mouth, and it mingled with the muskier flavour of his skin. Juliet did not doubt her own response. The thing had been warming and growing between them since that first evening's drinks at the new surgery and there was no reason to feel afraid or reluctant.

No room to feel those things either. Desire and warmth weakened her immediately, relaxing every muscle and sizzling in every nerve-ending. When his arms enveloped her more tightly, she lifted her own hands and found the firm hollow in the small of his back, then moved to explore the rippling pattern of muscles that webbed his capable torso. His fingers were threading through the thick fall of her russet hair now, and, when his kiss ended, it was only for a moment so that he could whisper fiercely, 'Gorgeous hair, so luscious and fragrant!' and bury his face in its bright strands.

Then their mouths met again and for a long time nothing existed but their two bodies entwined together in a rapture of discovery and pleasure giving.

Finally, though, he drew away from her. 'This is so tantalising. . .'

'I know,' she agreed, breathless and melting. 'Hugh, I. . . I think you should go.' She hardly recognised her own voice. Where had that husky note come from?

'I *know* I should go,' Hugh said. 'It's very hard. I think you'll have to push me out the door.'

'I'll try.' They moved towards it and she opened it, needing a hand grasping the round brass handle to support her desire-weakened limbs.

'Are you free tomorrow? We could take a picnic up into the hills. . .'

'I wish I *were* free,' she answered, still breathless with the speed of all this. 'But no, I have a barbecue with friends in Adelaide. It's all the way down at Christie's Beach, so by the time I get back. . .'

'Sunday afternoon, then?'

'Sunday would be wonderful.'

'I'll pick you up at two. We'll sit somewhere in a sunny café and have a Devonshire tea.'

'It sounds perfect.'

He started to bend towards her again then slowed the movement and whispered, 'I won't kiss you again. I can hear those twins already.' Then, as she laughed softly, his firm lips brushed feather-light against her own and he was gone, his footsteps making a gritty crunch on the stone-flagged veranda and the gravel path beyond. 'Goodnight, Juliet.' When he spoke, his tall silhouette was already blurred by the dark of the country night.

Tasting the tingle of that last ephemeral kiss still on her lips, and feeling it ripple outwards through her whole body like a pebble dropped in a still, deep pond, Juliet could manage only a husky-voiced, 'Bye.'

Inside, alone, she listened to the sound of his dark green Jaguar as it turned in the road and cruised smoothly away. Then a miaow and a purr at the open bedroom door told her that Spats, the old black and white puss she had brought with her from Adelaide, had awoken from a lazy two hours on the sheepskin rug beside the bed.

'Going to help me with the dishes, Spats?' she said aloud, but the cat was ready for night-time prowling and demanded to be let out of the back door.

Juliet put on some classical music, then, with her mind far away, she washed the few dishes that the simple meal had created. Her body was still alive with the memory of his kiss and when she thought of some of the things he had said as they ate she laughed aloud with pleasure. Sunday loomed like a bright jewel on the horizon of her future and there was the promise, too, of more days like it still to come, and of evenings like this one, so unexpected and delightful.

'I'm ready for this,' she said to herself. 'It's. . .it's magic.'

Her life had been too busy, too driven until now to really allow something like this into it. Men had asked her out but had not been able to get below the surface. Mostly her social life consisted of group events, like tomorrow's barbecue, where a cluster of couples and a floating collection of singles would get together to enjoy the open-air pleasures that the Australian climate

made so successful—picnics, barbecues, tennis afternoons, trips to the beach.

This thing with Hugh, she already felt, was different,
and as she slipped a cosy, lace-edged nightgown over
her smooth shoulders and let it fall softly over hips and
thighs she had no sense of foreboding about the future
. . .not even when she thought for the first time in
three hours about the fact that Hugh was David
Beckhill's cousin.

'It's windy, but if we wrap up warmly we'll be able to
enjoy those big clouds rolling along in the blue,' Hugh
said as Juliet opened the door to him two days later.

She nodded at his words. 'Yes, I love this sort of
day, actually. Really bracing—as long as my ears are
covered.'

'And spring is definitely in the air. The wattle is
stunning at the moment, against the backdrop of
winter-greened grass and racing sky.'

'But Mrs Radcliff hasn't had her twins?'

'No, more's the pity. If she was safely delivered I
really wouldn't have much to worry about. I don't have
anyone else due for another ten days. Then there's a
rash of them.'

'No reason to think any of them will go early?'

'Mrs Harden might. This is her second, and her first
one was quick off the mark apparently, two weeks
early. She wasn't my patient then.'

'But let's not spend the afternoon waiting for that
thing on your belt to go off.'

'No, let's not. I'm sure we'll find plenty to do
instead.' His eyes locked with hers and they both
smiled. The wind caught at his hair as they went down
the path together and Juliet thought how right it was,
those dark strands mixed with the threads of fine silver

at his temples. Thrusting hands deep into the pockets of the green wool jacket she wore above cream gabardine trousers, she surrendered herself to the pleasure of his company. It felt so comfortable, and yet sharply edged with something a little more dangerous and intoxicating as well.

'I feel as if I've known you for years,' she said, speaking the thought aloud as soon as it came to her.

He looked at her quizzically across the top of the Jaguar, whose gleaming forest-green paint matched her jacket almost perfectly. 'You have,' he said, a crooked smile disappearing inside the turned-up collar of his brown leather jacket.

The reminder sent a damp chill over her spirits suddenly, and she wished he had not pointed out her mistake. Technically it was true, and yet she felt so little continuity between that time and this that they might have been two different lives.

If Hugh was aware of her introspection, he didn't comment on it, although she noticed that on the first stretch of straight road he gave a sharp glance across at her from his position behind the wheel.

Will I say something? she wondered. Explain why I feel odd about it? No. That would only make it worse.

They drove through the village of Tavistock, with its cluster of surrounding wineries, and then left the comparative traffic jam of weekend wine-tasters to climb a winding road that led into the hills and south to the Mount Lofty Ranges. Hints of blossom were just beginning to appear on the rows of fruit trees that covered the softly folded slopes of hills and valleys, and craft shops and cafés were open in all the little towns.

After nearly an hour in which they spoke little except to point out something of scenic interest, Hugh slowed the vehicle. 'Like to park here and look in some of the craft galleries?' he suggested. 'There's a pottery here that's very good, and a place that does beautiful woodwork, glass, quilting. . . Then there's a café next door where it's possible to become very involved with chocolate.'

'Perfect, all of it,' Juliet laughed. Her awkwardness was gone again now, and their half-hour in the craft shops was full of delightful discoveries.

'These kaleidoscopes are wonderful,' she said at one point, holding a beautifully crafted brass tube to her eye and slowly turning the brass-rimmed circles at the far end so that the encrusting of rainbow-coloured glass created an endless series of patterns as it moved.

'Can I help you choose one?'

'Choose one? I couldn't just *buy* one!'

'Why not?'

'Because. . .' She stopped and laughed. 'I'm *not* going to buy one, but it is silly, isn't it? Frivolous luxuries like this have to be gifts, not cold-blooded selfish purchases on a whim. . . So I'll probably spend the next three years hinting and hoping in vain around every birthday.'

'When is your birthday?'

'October.'

'Not so very far away.'

'Careful! That's not supposed to be a comforting thought to a woman as soon as she's over the age of about twenty-three,' Juliet said as they moved away from the kaleidoscope display. 'We're supposed to dread each birthday as another step on the downward path.'

'Surely you don't feel that way?' He was more serious now.

'No, I don't,' she answered thoughtfully as they

stood together in front of some delicate, fluted glass-ware. 'If every year is rich and full—which is how my life has been so far, and I feel very lucky—I don't see what there is to regret in each one's passing.'

'Yes, I think an accumulation of empty years must do far more to make people afraid of growing older.' He nodded, then added more lightly, 'Had enough of crafts?'

'I think so, for today,' she answered. 'The town is quite crowded. All the café tables might be filled soon.'

'Why don't you go ahead, then, and reserve one for us? I've got a gift to buy.'

'You don't need any help in choosing it?'

'No, I don't,' he answered firmly, with a somewhat enigmatic smile.

He joined her in the café next door five minutes later, presenting her with a long, tissue-wrapped parcel as he sat in the chair opposite. For a horrible moment she thought he had interpreted her earlier words as a hint and had bought one of the lovely kaleidoscopes. It would be a gift far too extravagant for this casual occasion and she wouldn't know what to say. . . But as she took the package she realised that it was too light to be a kaleidoscope, and after she had unfurled the fragile tissue she found two tall thin candles that she had admired on first entering the craft shop, hand-dipped in several muted shades of grey and purple.

I should have know he'd pick just the right thing, she thought.

'To replace the ones we burned the other night over that very enjoyable meal,' he murmured.

'You'll have to come again, then, so you can enjoy these,' she answered.

'I'd like that very much.'

'Thank you, Hugh. They're beautiful.'

'And now. . .tea with scones and strawberry jam, or. . .?'

'Your description of the chocolate possibilities fired my imagination, actually.'

Half an hour later they were still lingering over coffee and wedges of wickedly rich Black Forest gateau.

'Would you like a refill?' The waitress spoke cheerily over Hugh's left shoulder and at that moment an ominous electric piping sound came from the pager clipped to his belt.

The two medical professionals looked at each other and Juliet grimaced. Hugh nodded ruefully and turned to the waitress. 'I think it'll have to be no,' he said, 'if this call is what I think. Is there a phone here I can use?'

He was back again very quickly.

'The twins?' Juliet asked, knowing what the answer would be.

'The twins,' he nodded. 'I've paid. Do you mind. . .?' He glanced down at the last unfinished mouthful of her cake.

'I couldn't,' she said. 'It was so wonderfully rich.'

'But I'm afraid. . . This is awful, but you're going to have to come to the hospital. Things are moving pretty fast, apparently, and I haven't got time to take that winding road back through the hills to drop you home. I'm a fool. I didn't think of the logistics of this when we planned the afternoon. I'm disappointed——'

'Please.' She touched his arm lightly as they squeezed through the door, past another couple on their way in. 'It's all right.'

He turned to her. 'No, it isn't,' he said softly. 'I was hoping I'd be able to kiss you again today and now there won't be time.'

As he spoke, he bent towards her and touched her lips, whispering the low words so that they became a caress against her mouth. Before she could respond, he had straightened again, but as they walked to the car his arm curved around her slim waist and when she laid her head against the hard strength of his shoulder she felt a deep warmth and contentment entwined with the sharper and headier awareness of desire.

'I'm sure you can ring for a taxi from the front desk,' Hugh said to Juliet as he swung the wheel of the green Jaguar and cruised to a smooth halt in his marked parking place near the hospital entrance.

He jumped out of the car at once without waiting for her reply and she had to hurry to unfasten her seatbelt, lock the passenger door and fall into step beside him.

'Actually,' she said a little breathlessly when she caught up. 'Would it be all right if I came with you to the obstetrics wing? I'll be starting to assist Margaret in giving childbirth classes two weeks from now and I know most couples have questions about the hospital. I've been wanting to see it for myself and talk to the staff.'

'Of course. Come along. I'll introduce you to Sister Barnes, who's in charge of labour and delivery today, and she'll pass you on to someone in the nursery and in post-natal as well.'

They passed through the main reception area and climbed two storeys in a spacious lift, then turned right to the largely self-contained wing where labour- and delivery-rooms, obstetrical operating theatre, post-partum recovery and nurseries were located.

This hospital, once a small regional centre, had expanded rapidly over the past two decades, as Adelaide's population spread northwards to form sub-

urbs from what had once been independent towns. The
Barossa Valley was at the northernmost end of the
hospital's catchment area, and Juliet knew that its
reputation was excellent in the field of obstetrics and
neo-natal care. Any obstetrical emergency could be
handled here, and only very premature or very ill
newborns had to be sent to the centre of Adelaide for
more sophisticated treatment.

'We'd both better wash,' Hugh said as they went
through the large door that separated this wing from
the rest of the hospital. 'You'd probably like to go into
one of the delivery-rooms if it's free, and of course
they're pretty strict about visitors' hygiene here.'

He ducked immediately into a washroom and Juliet
followed him, enjoying the atmosphere of importance
and activity that a hospital always exuded. It was more
than two years since she had last worked in a large
hospital environment like this one. You could get lost
in the size of the system at a place like this, but there
was a satisfaction to it, as well, that you didn't forget.

'It seems like a nice environment,' she said to Hugh
as they stood side by side, bending over the twin sinks
and soaping hands and forearms thoroughly.

'It is. I haven't spent much time here yet since I
don't really have a full complement of patients in the
new practice at this stage.'

'Actually, I've been surprised at how many deliveries
you *have* had this week.'

'Several patients decided to stay with me and deliver
here when they found I was moving. They lived in the
Salisbury or Elizabeth area, so it wasn't much further
to come. And a few women have transferred to me
from Dr Gordon or Dr Steinbeck. Almost all our
patients are happy to be seen by any of the three of us,
which means we can take it in turns to have a weekend

free from those midnight calls. Unfortunately, this wasn't mine.'

Their eyes met via the mirror in front of them and she read the frank desire in his expression, feeling her cheeks glow and her heart begin to race. He smiled, and traces of fine wrinkles fanned at the corners of his hazel eyes. His long lashes were dark crescents on his lightly tanned skin and his fine, strong nose anchored his face in serious planes. Juliet remembered how that nose had bumped lightly against her own on Friday night as they kissed, and for the first time she knew a moment of fear and doubt. This was too nice, too easy, and it was happening too fast.

He pulled a length of crisp, clean linen from the dispenser on the wall and dried his hands. 'I must go. If I don't see you. . . I'll see you tomorrow.'

'Yes. Hope it goes well.'

He left the washroom as she moved to dry her own hands and she found it hard to part from him with such a casual exchange, although she told herself very firmly that an obstetrician about to deliver twins could scarcely spend time on romantic farewells. A minute later, she left the washroom herself.

'Juliet?' A brunette of about her own age came towards her along the short corridor before she had closed the door behind her. 'Dr Beckhill said you wanted to see over our set-up.'

'Yes.' She explained quickly about the childbirth classes and the other nurse nodded.

'Yes, it helps so much if the couples know what to expect. Some of them come through on our tours, but we don't have the staff to give those as often as we'd like to. The last one was in June, I think, nearly two months ago. And of course not everyone is free to

come on the afternoon we set aside. I'm Jenny Barnes,
by the way.'

She led Juliet to the nurses' station, which was
centrally located between three labour-rooms, a more
informal birthing-room, two delivery-rooms, and the
operating theatre and post-partum recovery.

'It seems quiet today,' Juliet said, noting that the
three labour-rooms were all empty.

'Yes, we had one about an hour ago and she's still in
recovery with her baby. There was a Caesar just before
I came on, too, but now there's only Mrs Radcliff and
her twins.'

'They must be in the birthing-room.'

'Yes, and things are going pretty well. She was six
centimetres dilated when I examined her, just before
Dr Beckhill arrived, and she's nice and relaxed and
working well on her breathing. Anyway, it means I can
come round with you and tell you anything you want
to know. You've done mid, haven't you?'

'Yes, at Princess Alexandra.'

'I've never been there. I trained in Melbourne, but
I'm very keen on what we have here. Let's start with
the labour-rooms, shall we?'

The three generous-sized rooms were side by side
and all much the same, painted in a restful pale blue
with small adjoining bathrooms. Juliet noted the monitors which would show foetal heart-rate as well as a
print-out that indicated the strength and timing of each
contraction.

'Mostly the women are able to walk around but once
they are ready to lie down and be put on IV fluids
these monitors are very helpful. The husbands can see
the shape of each contraction and tell their wives when
the pain is about to diminish, often before she's aware
of it herself.'

'Some couples would prefer less technology, though, wouldn't they?' Juliet said.

'The birthing-room fits the bill for them, then—although some of this equipment is available there, too, if they want it.'

'And what's the hospital policy on intervention procedures—episiotomy, induction and that sort of thing?'

'The hospital policy is that it's between doctors and patients, but less intervention is to be encouraged. It really varies. Dr Gordon is rather old-school—oh, of course, he's head partner in your practice, isn't he?'

'Yes, but I haven't worked much with him, yet. Margaret Chatham usually deals with his patients.'

'Well, you'll soon find out the differences in approach among your three. And of course Dr Beckhill's style is fairly new to us here.'

They left the labour-room, still talking shop and finding an easy rapport which would probably come in handy at times, since they were bound to speak by phone reasonably often. Then, as they made their way around to the delivery-rooms and theatre, Hugh emerged from the birthing-room, closing the door behind him with a careful click. He saw the two nurses at once.

'Enjoying your tour?' He touched Juliet lightly on the arm and she saw Jenny Barnes give a curious glance. Hugh had seen it too, and he drew away quickly to turn to the other nurse. 'She's seven and a half centimetres already, Sister Barnes, so it looks like it won't be long. The foetal heart-rates are both good, no sign of distress, and the mother's energy is holding out well. We should be able to deliver safely in the birthing-room. I'm going to drop in on pre-natal to visit Mrs Jennings and Mrs Arden.'

'Jenny. . .' An anxious junior appeared at that

moment. 'I just took a call from downstairs. Two new admissions on their way.'

'Two?' Jenny turned apologetically to Juliet. 'It's always like this, isn't it? There'll probably be another one in half an hour. I'll have to go.'

'Of course,' Juliet nodded.

'Not my patients, I take it,' Hugh put in.

'No,' the junior said. 'At least. . .' She looked questioningly at Sister Barnes.

'I'll check for you, Noela,' the senior said reassuringly to the second-year student. 'They're probably not private patients, so. . .'

She left with pixie-faced Noela after another grimace of apology to Juliet.

'Would you like me to continue your tour?' Hugh asked, touching her once again, this time with a light palm against the small of her back. His hand was instantly warm against her, sending a thrill of desire like a throbbing pulse, but his touch was gone almost as soon as it came.

'Have you got time?' she answered him, suppressing a gasp. 'Your patients. . .'

'You'd like to see the post-partum ward as well, wouldn't you?'

'Yes.'

'Then it's easy. Here are the delivery-rooms. We'll look at those on the way.'

He ushered her into one of the empty, spotlessly clean and tidy, and very brightly lit rooms. It was equipped with monitoring equipment for both mother and baby, including a special heated crib where the baby's condition could be carefully checked when it was only a few minutes old, and rated according to a scale known as the Apgar score. 'There are mirrors if the mother wants to see the baby emerging——'

'I imagine a lot of women don't!'

He laughed and nodded. 'Although a lot of couples bring a camera, these days. Most patients here are very satisfied with the choices they're given, according to surveys taken over the past two years. The theatre is a little more complex than these two rooms, of course. We won't go in, but you can see the set-up though this window. And again, we try to give the patient a choice of epidural or general anaesthesia whenever possible. The quality of epidural anaesthesia has improved so much over the past ten years, so I usually encourage my patients to take that option. Dr Gordon doesn't,' he added in a slightly different tone.

'I can imagine some people would be nervous about the idea of being conscious during major surgery.'

'Of course, but when you talk about this during the childbirth classes do point out the advantages. The husband can be present, and the mother can see her baby as soon as it's born. It feels much more like a natural birth than going to sleep, waking up all groggy and first seeing your baby anything up to eight hours later.'

'Why is Dr Gordon less keen on it, then? I'm not playing devil's advocate,' Juliet added hastily, 'it's just that I have to work with both of you, so I need to understand both angles.'

But Hugh only shrugged. 'You should probably ask him. We haven't discussed the subject in any depth.'

He spoke cheerfully enough, but Juliet suddenly wondered if there could be friction in future in the new partnership, between Hugh's vigorous new approach and Dr Gordon's more conservative ways. Aware of how important her own role was in smoothing over this kind of problem, she stored the matter carefully away in her mind.

Next they came to the nurseries, where nearly a dozen tiny bundles lay in wheeled cribs. Afternoon visiting hour had just begun, so there were several people standing eagerly at the big glass windows peering at the new little beings in their lives. Most of the babies were in the large nursery on the right of the corridor, but on the left a smaller room, more dominated by the latest medical equipment, contained two tiny premature babies, who would need special care for several days and perhaps weeks until they reached a healthy weight and were permitted to go home.

'It must be hard on the parents,' Juliet murmured, looking at the smallest of the babies, who was attached to sensitive instruments which monitored her heart-rate and breathing constantly.

'Hard on the doctor, too, as far as I'm concerned,' Hugh said. 'I always feel there should have been a way to stop the baby from being born until the right time. It's incredible that no matter how sophisticated our neo-natal intensive care gets—and this premmie nursery isn't as intensive as some, and passes a baby on to Adelaide if it's really small or ill—it still can't match the environment of the womb.'

'I wish the care of premmie babies didn't have to be so impersonal,' Juliet said. 'Look at all this equipment. I know it's necessary, but. . .'

'Perhaps it isn't as necessary as we think,' Hugh murmured.

'How do you mean?'

They were still standing together in front of the nursery window and Juliet had the disturbing realisation that they must look just like two new parents. Her question to him was as much an attempt to keep her emotional equilibrium right now as anything else.

'Medical studies are starting to show that human

touch helps babies to thrive as much as the best diet and hygiene and monitoring,' he said. 'I suspect that's what good mothers have known underneath all along. If neo-natal care was my field, I'd certainly want to explore the question. As it's not, however, I confine myself to doing what I can to keep those pre-term babies inside their mothers where they belong.'

They had been speaking in low voices, not wanting to intrude with their medical talk on the visitors' enjoyment of the babies, and now a small silver-haired woman looked up at them and smiled. 'Which one's yours?'

I was right, Juliet thought. We *do* look like parents.

Stupidly, she found that she was blushing as Hugh answered with a light laugh. 'They're *all* ours! I'm waiting for a patient to deliver me two more right now.'

'Two more. . .? Oh, silly me!' the elderly lady replied, flustered. 'I didn't take in your coat and name badge. Don't let me keep you, but. . .that's my first grandson in the middle there, in the other nursery. Did you deliver him?'

'Let's see. . . Daniel Hanson,' Hugh read aloud from the card attached to the foot of the crib. 'No, I didn't. He's beautiful, though. Congratulations!'

He smiled again and steered Juliet towards the post-natal ward, where the mothers of the dozen newborns rested in two-bed rooms grouped around a central nursing station and bathroom facilities. 'I must get in to see Mrs Jennings and Mrs Arden,' he said. 'Those twins aren't going to wait around. We've been away longer than I intended.'

'It was the nurseries,' Juliet laughed. 'I've experienced it before when I was at Princess Alexandra. You always spend longer in front of those windows than you plan to.'

'Yes, even hardened professionals like ourselves. Here, this is Sister Jolley over here. I'll leave you with her and she'll show you around. . .and this time I really will say goodbye, Juliet, and leave you to that taxi, because by the time I finish in here. . .'

'I know,' she nodded firmly. 'Don't apologise. It's fine. Go.'

He took a quick look at the nurses' station and along the corridor, then ducked towards her and left a brief, caressing kiss burning on her lips. When he straightened, Denise Jolley had caught sight of him and was coming over.

It's the end, Juliet realised. Only the end of the afternoon with Hugh, she told herself. Nothing so very tragic. I'll see him at work tomorrow. And yet she could not rid herself, somehow, of the fear that tomorrow it would all be different.

CHAPTER FOUR

'I WANT the test re-done,' David Beckhill seethed, out of Juliet's sight as she put down fresh towelling on the examination bench, but by no means out of earshot. He was closeted in Hugh's office and the atmosphere was electric.

'David, you're being an idiot.' Hugh's response was patient and heavy.

'Am I, indeed?'

'Yes. I said the sperm count was a little lower than——'

'I don't need to stay and listen to this patronising rubbish you're spouting, Hugh.'

'David, wait, shouldn't you be thinking about Alicia——?'

But the abrupt slam of the door told Juliet that David Beckhill hadn't stayed to hear his cousin's words. Listening to Hugh's angry pacing, Juliet waited a minute then knocked quietly at the connecting door. Aware of the growing backlog of patients in the waiting-room, she knew that she really had to help get things moving.

'Come in!' came Hugh's absent command.

'I think we really need to close those transom windows, Hugh,' she said to him on entering. 'I know Dr Gordon says it helps the building to heat evenly, and we'll probably want it for cool air flow in summer, but. . .'

'I know. No privacy for scenes like the one you just

undoubtedly overheard,' Hugh nodded tersely. Then, in a clear dismissal of the subject, 'Who's waiting?'

'Mrs Arkin's next, then Vickie Davis and a new patient, Felicity Jaeger. She's here for a pregnancy test and has just gone to give us a specimen,' she summarised quickly.

'Good. Thanks, Juliet,' he nodded, again a little absently.

She went to the waiting-room to summon Mrs Arkin, chastising herself inwardly for the disappointment she felt. It was Wednesday now, and Hugh had been so businesslike all week. Friendly, but businesslike. Had something gone wrong already, with their happy discovery of each other that had begun over the weekend? We've been so busy. . .she thought, not knowing if it was grasping at straws to think that way. 'Mrs Arkin?' she called across the large room, and a woman of about thirty rose with a rather wan smile and came forward. She was in the early stages of pregnancy, and perhaps that accounted for the pallor and listlessness. . . No, it was more than that. 'Is anything the matter?'

'I'm all right.' But tears had overflowed and were muffling the woman's speech. Wavy light brown hair hung on either side of her face as she dropped her head in a vain attempt to conceal rapidly reddening eyes.

'Do tell the doctor about it if anything is troubling you,' Juliet insisted gently, and Mrs Arkin nodded.

'I will. It's just. . . I'm having a bit of bleeding and I've already had one miscarriage. . .'

'Here's Dr Beckhill. He'll find out what's going on,' Juliet said, guiding Mrs Arkin to the examination bench then quietly closing the door and leaving doctor and patient alone. A few minutes later, Dr Beckhill called her as she was running the new patient's pregnancy test.

'I've taken an HCG titer,' he said. 'Make sure it goes at lunchtime with the rest of the path lab things. We'll take another one next week and check the difference in HCG levels. Vickie Davis will be with me for a while, so if you could answer any questions that Mrs Arkin has about the test while you take her blood-pressure. . .'

'Of course.' She slipped past him into the examination-room and felt the light brush of his forearm against her own, an accidental touch but one that set her pulses racing uncontrollably. Then, so briefly that she might almost have imagined it, came the deliberate trailing of his fingertips across the back of her hand, and her spirits rose into the clouds with dangerous swiftness.

Mrs Arkin had dressed again after the internal examination. Glancing quickly at the patient's notes, Juliet saw that Dr Beckhill had found evidence of continuing bleeding, although he had noted that it was very slight. There was little to say to comfort the woman. Although trying to remain calm, she was obviously upset about the bleeding, and until the results of the first test and the follow-up next Tuesday were known complete reassurance could not honestly be given.

'Dr Beckhill says he didn't have time to fully explain the test to you,' she said to Mrs Arkin in a gentle yet matter-of-fact tone. Often it didn't help at times like this if the medical staff gave too much sympathy that needed to come from closer to home. Patsy Arkin obviously didn't want to cry on anyone's shoulder here today.

'No, he didn't,' she managed. 'It's to test whether I'm still really pregnant, isn't it?'

'Sort of,' Juliet answered. 'HCG is a hormone that is

produced by the placenta and the brain when you're pregnant, and it should rise steadily as the pregnancy goes through its early stages. Human chorionic gonadotropin is its full name. A terrible mouthful, so we don't use it very often. If the conceptus isn't viable—and that's the most common reason for early miscarriage——'

'Yes, people said that to me last time. Nature's way of letting a damaged baby go. 'It. . .it doesn't help, actually, to hear that at the time.'

'No, I know,' Juliet said carefully. 'But it helps later. I just want to make sure you understand the aim of the test. If the baby isn't developing any more, the HCG level won't have risen next time we take your blood. It's a way of knowing more quickly what is going on, and it means we can start gathering the information we'll need to start treating a long-term problem. Please try to remember, though, that the odds are in your favour. Nearly a third of first pregnancies end in miscarriage, for one reason or another, and most women go on to have a lovely healthy baby next time round. Bleeding happens in a lot of very healthy pregnancies and Dr Beckhill says yours is very slight. It's very likely that the next test result will show a good jump in the HCG level, and you can stop worrying.'

'I feel so helpless, though. Just waiting till the test, or till. . .like last time. . .'

'Can you take things easy for the next few days?'

'Yes, Dr Beckhill told me that, and I can take time off work.'

'Good, and lie down whenever you can, on your left side with a pillow under your legs. That will send the strongest blood supply to the uterus and the developing baby. And if you enjoy herbal teas, some people believe in a cup or two of raspberry tea to help a pregnancy along. Medical science won't promise it helps, but we know it doesn't hurt.'

'I'll do anything to get rid of this helpless feeling.'

'And telephone any time anything happens, or if you remember any questions we didn't answer today.'

'Thank you, Sister. I'm sorry I was upset. . .'

'Don't be silly!'

'And I feel a lot better now. You've really helped.'

'Well, I hope so. I know it's hard when you just have to wait.'

The rest of the morning was a pattern of typical ups and downs. A patient of Dr Gordon's was found, on undergoing a sonogram, to be carrying triplets, a patient of Dr Beckhill's with fertility problems had a positive pregnancy test at last, and a patient of Dr Steinbeck's, who had been having increasingly heavy bleeding for the past five days, did lose her baby in the eighth week of pregnancy.

At lunchtime, Hugh left for the day, as it was his regular afternoon off. Juliet's time was now divided between Dr Steinbeck and Dr Gordon, and she couldn't help noticing that, again, the waiting-room seemed to be full of pregnant bellies or tiny newborns when a new patient arrived to see Dr Gordon for the first of what might be a long series of tests to determine the reason for her infertility.

I wonder if Hugh has talked to Dr Gordon about scheduling infertility patients at special times, she thought. I should remind him.

It was a slightly painful series of thoughts, reminding her as it did of Hugh's scene with David this morning, and of the fact that the obstetrician had gone off once again with no special sign or word. . .

Or had he? 'Did you see the note Dr Beckhill left for you?' Debbie said at the end of the day as the last

patient departed and files were returned to drawers
and magazine tables tidied.

'Note? No, I didn't.' Juliet heard the thinness in her
tone and hoped that the efficient and observant secretary hadn't picked up on it.

'Sorry. I meant to mention it hours ago, but I've
been on the phone half the day.' She ran her fingers
through a halo of curly light brown hair in mock
despair. 'Eleven people wanted to change their
appointments for next week. It's funny how these
things either come in droves or not at all.' With the
tips of two busy fingers she picked a folded sheet of
yellow message paper from Juliet's pigeonhole and
reached across the desktop with it. 'Here!'

'Thanks.' Juliet forced herself to speak normally.
This sudden weakness in her legs was utterly ridiculous!
'It's probably just a reminder about something we
were. . .' She trailed off incoherently and was relieved
to see that Debbie had already turned to something
else.

Waiting until she was safely outside, she finally
opened the note, standing in the late-afternoon sun
and leaning against the warm, polished blue side of her
small car.

'I'll ring you tonight at home—Hugh' was all it said,
but somehow the words had the power to send a tingle
of happiness and anticipation all through her.

Once at the cottage after the smooth country drive,
it was hard to concentrate on the trivial business of
end-of-day tasks. She fed Spats, watered the seven
African violets that were blooming in an array of
mauves and purples on the sunny kitchen windowsill,
scribbled a light-hearted birthday message in a card for
a friend in Adelaide, and made vegetable soup and a
toasted cheese sandwich for her evening meal. All this

time, the phone stayed silent and she had to scold herself more than once for the way her eyes kept straying to it while her mind willed it to burst into life.

When it did finally ring, she had just switched on the television and got out the lacy baby's matinée jacket that she was knitting for a new godchild. It'll be Mother from Perth. She hasn't phoned in over two weeks, and she usually rings at this time of night, Juliet thought firmly, and she had convinced herself so thoroughly of this that when she heard Hugh's masculine baritone she stuttered stupidly, 'Oh. . .hi. . .yes, hello, Hugh,' and felt like a complete fool.

'We've haven't had a chance to talk all week,' he said. 'And anyway, I'm sure you don't want to mix business with pleasure any more than I do.'

'No, of course not,' she agreed automatically. Why were her pulses racing at the mere sound of his voice? She sat on the low stool by the telephone table and tried to anchor herself more firmly to good sense.

'Mind if I drop in for a quick cup of coffee? I'm just on my way home from the hospital.'

'Of course you can drop in. I even have some cake to go with the coffee.'

'I won't get to you for another half-hour—that won't be too late?'

'It's only half-past eight now.'

'See you, then.'

A click disconnected them and she gave a brief, slightly shaky laugh then spoke aloud to Spats, who had just come out of the bedroom. 'He's coming round, Puss, and I want to go and put on silk and sequins. I'm falling in love with Hugh Beckhill and it feels wonderful.' She scooped the cat into her arms and felt the vibrating engine of his purr. 'Spats, it's terrible! What am I going to do?'

Burrowing his furred face against her shoulder, Spats clearly didn't think there was a problem. Juliet, however, studying her pink cheeks and shining eyes in the mirror five minutes later as she brushed her hair into a glossy halo and renewed long-disappeared cinnamon-pink lipstick, couldn't be so blasé.

When Hugh arrived half an hour later, she had coffee just brewed and Spats reluctantly banished for an early start to his night of hunting. A cinnamon coffee cake sat on a plate on the coffee-table, and the doctor caught sight of it at once.

'I guarantee I'll manage at least three pieces of that if it's not rationed,' he said.

Noting the slightly tired appearance of his dark trousers and blue shirt, Juliet said, 'You were supposed to have the afternoon off. Don't tell me you were called in, *and* you've skipped dinner!'

''Fraid so. Complications with some surgery. A woman with endometriosis. I was called in to cover another surgeon's mistake, and——Anyway,' he interrupted himself, 'I don't want to indulge in shop talk and I'm sure you don't want to listen to it.'

'Of course I don't!' she answered. 'I want to get you something to eat that's more substantial than cake!'

'Cake is fine.'

'Cake is *not* very nutritious!'

They faced each other in mock hostility over the coffee-table until he ended the exchange with a burst of rich laughter. 'Juliet, what I really want most is. . .'

He didn't finish the statement in words. Instead, he reached over and pulled her towards him, shifting the coffee-table neatly aside with one knee and surrounding her with strong, commanding arms. She went to him willingly, heart thudding and skin already tingling at his warm touch. Their lips met, gently at first, with a slow teasing exploration, then as his arms tightened around her and his hands began to find the curves and hidden places of her ripe figure her mouth began to feel swollen and numbed by the hungry pressure of his.

It was a long time before they drew apart, slowly and unwillingly, but each realised that the next step would be dangerously easy to take.

'The coffee must be getting cold,' Juliet said shakily, turning to the silver pot on the table in order to hide flaming cheeks and lips that could still seek out his mouth again with the slightest encouragement.

Willing her hands to remain steady, she picked up a fragile white cup and poured in the dark liquid, happy to see that it still steamed richly. Time must be playing tricks. Each moment had felt fathomless in his arms.

'Thanks,' he said briefly when she held the cup out to him and coaxed him to sit, with a wordless gesture. 'This wasn't why I came,' he went on, after a pause.

'Wasn't it?' Her glance flicked towards him and she frowned. What was this?

He laughed ruefully. 'That came out very badly. What I mean is, I wanted. . . I want. . . Juliet, you're robbing me of the power of speech, do you know that?'

'Strange,' she murmured, 'I feel a bit that way myself. It must be contagious.'

'I want to ask you out again this weekend, but I have a lot on. . .'

'That's all right,' she answered, a too-light tone doing more to emphasise her disappointment in her own ears than to hide it. 'I'm pretty busy, too.'

'Are you?' But was that disappointment she heard in his own voice? 'Because I was going to say. . .there's Friday night.'

'Friday? Yes, I'm free then.'

'Excellent! But I want an honest answer from you.

It's a formal dinner at the Beckhill Estate. If you'd feel too uncomfortable about it because of David. . . You see, this is why I didn't want to simply toss out an invitation over the phone.'

David again. Not for the first time, she felt awkward at the reminder. Her ex-fiancé seemed to be hovering over this fragile new blossoming like a ghost. A spurt of anger rose in her throat suddenly, so that her next words came out more bluntly and abruptly than she had intended, and her closed fists were pressed tightly against her thighs as she stared almost unseeingly in front of her.

'That was far too squeamish of you, Hugh,' she said on a harsh note. 'Or at least, you're assuming feelings in me that I don't possess at all. I'd like to spend Friday evening with you very much and the fact that it happens to be at the Beckhill Estate is neither here nor there, so please don't tiptoe around the subject like this again!'

She continued to stare down at the coffee-table, waiting for his response, and only looked up when his silence had lasted for an uncomfortable space of time. He had drawn away, she found. Hardly surprising. Her outburst had been unreasonable. . .and not even the truth, the voice of conscience whispered insistently at the back of her mind.

'All right,' he answered slowly at last. 'It's. . .good to know how you really feel. I wasn't sure before, and now I am.'

'Good. It's always best to be frank, isn't it?' she said, her voice as brittle as glass now. There had been a double edge to his words and she felt the sense of closeness and comfort between them evaporating like thin morning mist.

'Yes.' He turned to face her again, having completed

an inspection of the quaint collection of ornaments—
gathered over the years from a dozen unlikely
sources—that were arranged on the mantelpiece above
the fireplace.

It seemed fitting, somehow, that she hadn't lit a fire
tonight, and that last week's golden daffodils had
crumpled at the edges and been thrown away. The
stone hearth was dark and chilly, and so was the
mantelpiece above, like the unspoken mood that had
suddenly grown between them over these past few
minutes.

'Anyway,' he went on, 'I'd better give you the
details. It's a rather formal affair, as I said. That means
dinner suits and glamorous dresses, and we should
arrive pretty punctually at a quarter to eight. So shall I
pick you up here at half-past seven?'

'That sounds fine,' she nodded. 'I'm glad it's not too
early, since it's formal. I'll have plenty of time to
change after work.'

'Yes, I always need a good hot shower after a long
day with patients. In fact, just saying the words makes
me hunger for one right now. Do you mind if I pass on
the coffee and cake after all, Juliet?'

'Of course not,' she murmured.

What had happened? Was it just because she had
been abrupt that the mood was now so awkward and
superficial? Surely not! He's just tired, she said to
herself desperately. I won't make it worse by demanding an explanation. Everything will be all right again
on Friday.

He was already halfway to the door, but she darted
up beside him and opened it, less out of hostessly
courtesy than because she need a prop—something to
do with her hands, a solid wooden support to lean
against and hide behind.

'Thanks,' he said automatically as he passed her and stepped out into the night. Then he turned and gave her a long, assessing look, which she could only meet as steadily as possible. 'Goodnight, Juliet.' He bent towards her, but if he had intended to kiss her he changed his mind before the intention became a reality.

Instead, he held himself back and, frowning thoughtfully, brushed his fingers gently along her jawline. Her lips, already parted and ripe to receive his kiss, felt numb and clumsy as she answered him, 'Goodnight, Hugh. See you tomorrow.'

'Yes. Sleep well.'

'You too,' she said. A polite formula. Perhaps he *would* sleep well. He looked tired enough to need ten hours in bed. For herself, she doubted that rest would come so easily.

'The results of Wednesday morning's tests are in from the path lab,' Debbie Miller reported just after lunch on Friday.

'I'll run through them and see if there's anything that needs to be reported straight away,' Juliet offered, since she had a spare moment after returning from her half-hour lunch break.

She took the test print-outs and sat down to look through them. Mrs Arkin's HCG titer was the last thing she came to, and although only a doctor was fully qualified to interpret the result she knew enough to see that the figures indicating the HCG level looked much higher than Dr Beckhill had feared. She turned back to Debbie. 'These others can wait till the patients phone us for the result,' she said, 'But this last one I'll take in to Dr Beckhill now.'

The last words were spoken with a mixture of firmness and breeziness, and now that she had stated her intention aloud Juliet knew that she had to go through with it.

'He's still on the phone, I think,' Debbie said. 'Hang on. . . Yes, the red light's still on. . . No, wait. He's free. Go now, because I can see his next patient coming up the path.'

'OK,' Juliet replied lightly, angry at herself. These stupid flutterings inside! She had seen Hugh a dozen times today already, and two dozen times yesterday. He had been perfectly friendly, hadn't mentioned Wednesday night, or tonight's formal dinner at the Beckhill Estate. Why this reluctance to speak to him? Her sense of distance from him was surely just imagination.

Swallowing personal concerns firmly at last, she took Mrs Arkin's file and knocked on Hugh's office door, then entered at his brief invitation.

'Mrs Arkin's test result was in the batch that just arrived from the path lab,' she said. 'I thought you should see it straight away.'

'Bad?' he frowned, half rising in the leather swivel chair behind the desk and reaching out for the sheet of paper she held.

'Actually, the opposite, from my reading. That HCG level is very good for this stage in her pregnancy, isn't it?'

'Let's see.' The paper snapped in his hand as he took it and sat down. Juliet stood there, studying his reaction. 'You've got her file with you?'

'Yes. Here.' Again, she held it out, almost at arm's length, wanting to go closer but afraid to make any gesture that he might interpret as personal. The hard, tanned shape of his wrist emerging from an immaculate white shirt cuff was only one of the parts of him that she instantly longed to touch and explore.

'Now. . . I seem to remember she was pretty certain of her dates,' he muttered thoughtfully as he studied the file and the test result. A few moments later he looked up and smiled, meeting her eyes frankly for the first time since Wednesday. 'Yes, you're right! This is a great result. Phone her and tell her I'm not even going to do the follow-up test. With the HCG level this high at this stage, that pregnancy has to be going strong.'

'I'll phone her right now.'

'Good. . . Got your dress ready for tonight?'

The abrupt change of subject took her by surprise and she stammered a little as she replied. 'Y-yes, I have.' She didn't confess that she had made a panicky dash to Adelaide after work yesterday to buy something suitable.

'I'm looking forward to it.'

'The dress?' she returned archly, daring to be humorous in her relief that the coolness she had detected— or imagined—had gone now.

'Certainly,' he drawled, a teasing smile parting his well-moulded lips slightly. 'But even more to what's inside it. . . Is there a patient waiting?'

'Need you even ask?'

She left the room on the harmonious chord of their shared laughter, and walked through the rest of the day on light feet, scarcely minding that her work brought her into contact mainly with the other two obstetricians in the practice. Tonight, she would see Hugh alone again.

It was only a few minutes before she was due to leave when the call came from an older first-time mother, Penny Smythe.

'Her waters have broken but she's had no pains yet,' Juliet reported to Hugh over the internal phone line. 'I told her to come in straight away, but she wants to wait twenty minutes until her husband gets home from work.'

'All right,' he answered, with the calmness of someone well-used to having plans altered at the last minute.

'Does this mean. . .?' She hesitated. Debbie was just beside her at the reception desk, and the day's last patient was still getting her things in the waiting-room. Should their blossoming relationship be kept secret at work? It certainly seemed a wise idea to be cautious.

'Tonight?' he guessed correctly.

'Yes.'

'It shouldn't be a problem. Vern and Geoffrey are covering for me this weekend—which technically starts at six according to the rules of this practice. I'll examine her here but Geoffrey will take over once she gets to the hospital. Don't worry,' he added in a quieter tone. 'You won't be disappointed.'

'Good,' she said carefully, making the monosyllable as tender as she dared.

As she said her goodnight to Debbie it was hard to hide the happiness that had taken hold of her, a flooding tide of it that buoyed her up and made her want to sing and laugh and pour out the secret of this new feeling to whoever would listen.

Perhaps there was no need to pour it out. Perhaps it was quite obvious to everyone. 'You must have something special on this weekend,' Margaret said as they left the building together and crossed the chilly gravel of the small parking area to their cars on the far side. 'You're almost dancing.'

'Am I?' Juliet prevaricated unsuccessfully.

'Yes! You make me feel quite staid and ancient by comparison. It must be someone quite wonderful.'

'It. . . Well, yes, he is,' Juliet answered. Somehow it was very hard to lie about being happy!

'I thought so,' Margaret nodded, pleased with her guess. 'Yours is a name that has to bring romance, and, with your looks and personality, I was sure there had to be someone special.'

'Oh, he's not very special yet,' Juliet answered awkwardly, then went on in a rush, 'I mean, he is, but it's too early to. . .'

'Is it? I won't pester, then. See you on Monday!' As good as her word, Margaret said a brief goodbye then climbed into her matronly yellow vehicle, leaving Juliet already regretting that she had given away so much.

Nobody must guess that it's Hugh, she thought as she drove away. At least. . .not yet.

CHAPTER FIVE

'DID you think I wasn't coming after all?' The lazy drawl came from the dimly lit veranda as Juliet opened the door at five to eight.

'Almost,' she breathed. 'Come in.'

'No, I'd rather stay here where I can see you silhouetted against the light. . . And anyway, we should be going. I'm sorry I'm late, and I should have phoned, but it seemed quickest just to get ready as fast as I could and turn up. That's a stunning dress.'

'Thank you.'

'And just right for tonight.'

'I was afraid it might be *too* formal, but——'

'But then you remembered that glittering formality is very much in the Beckhill tradition. Too much so, I sometimes think,' he added lightly.

Juliet made no reply. His compliment on her dress had partially repaid its extravagance. The fitted bodice and long sleeves in cream silk taffeta encrusted with tiny black beads and sequins enhanced the curves of her figure perfectly, the skirt that fell to the floor in layers of the same cream silk made a luxurious rustle as she walked, and the wide, curved neckline that scooped to below her neat shoulder-blades in the back made the perfect setting for a simple necklace of black onyx and gold, but a dress like this did not come cheaply.

Since buying it yesterday she had blown hot and cold, one minute almost ashamed of the gaping hole it had made in her credit-card balance, the next minute not counting the cost at all because she knew she needed a dress like this to feel fully comfortable about the evening that lay ahead. Now, as Hugh spoke so lightly of 'the Beckhill tradition', she realised that a mere dress could not be armour enough. Ghosts of the past were crowding in, and if Hugh didn't stand beside her with the right kind of support the hours ahead might be gruelling ones.

She wanted to reach out and take his arm, ask for his reassurance, say to him, 'If things get difficult, be prepared to rescue me, won't you?', but somehow it was too soon to presume that kind of intimacy. Instead, once he had opened the door for her so she could arrange her silk skirts without creasing their luxurious layers, and they were moving smoothly along the dark country road, she asked, 'Nothing wrong tonight, was there? You hadn't expected to be so long.'

'No, nothing wrong,' he answered easily. 'By the time Mr Smythe got home from work, Penny's pains had speeded up quite a bit. I told her to skip coming to the office. I sent her straight to the hospital and met her there. Then Vern turned up to see another patient and we. . .talked and I lost track of time. But that's the last bit of shop talk for tonight, all right?'

'All right,' she laughed, although she noticed that his change of subject seemed rather abrupt and wished he hadn't put the taboo on medical topics quite so soon. She would have liked to probe a little on the subject of his 'talk' with Vern Gordon. Why the pause, for exampe, before the word?

Fifteen minutes later, the pillared gates of the Beckhill estate loomed in front of them. Floodlit from behind, with a glow that drowned the headlights of the car, the entrance was inviting but at the same time frighteningly imposing. The low Jaguar swept straight

in without a pause. A uniformed gatekeeper guarded
the estate entrance tonight, and his brief gesture that
was half-wave, half-salute showed that he recognised
Hugh and his vehicle immediately. Once again, Juliet
found it unsettling. At seventeen, in spite of her own
then well-to-do circumstances, she had been thrilled
and awed, on arriving here in David's car, by this same
guarded gate and winding gravelled driveway—thrilled
because she had expected to live in these regal sur-
roundings one day, and awed the way Cinderella must
have been awed at finding herself the belle of the ball.
Now, of course, she had no such expectations, and no
desire, either, to be the centre of attention at tonight's
affair.

'Who. . .how many people are expected tonight?'
she blurted nervously to Hugh as the house loomed
into view. It, too, was floodlit, and this made it seem
even larger than Juliet had remembered, with its wide,
pillared veranda on three sides, large suite of reception
rooms, upper two floors of bedrooms and bathrooms,
and extension of kitchen and staff facilities out the
back. Beyond the house, the darker unlit shapes of the
winery buildings could just be seen—the cellars, the
processing plants, and the tasting rooms that the public
reached by another entrance.

'How many?' Hugh was saying. 'About two hundred,
I think. As to *who*——'

'Two *hundred*!' she gasped in horror.

'Yes.' He glanced across at her, evidently surprised
at her reaction. 'I told you it was to be very formal,
didn't I?'

'Yes, but a formal dinner can be for eight.'

'Not according to Uncle Lloyd's way of thinking. I
thought you would remember that.'

'I didn't, I'm afraid.'

'And the idea throws you? It didn't used to. You always seemed to relish glittering throngs.'

This was too much. 'Hugh!' she burst out, the silk of her dress rustling as she shifted in the low car seat, agitated and verging on anger. 'Must you keep on reminding me about the fact that I've been here before? Things are very different now. I've changed. I thought you knew that. . .could see it. One minute you're treading on tiptoe around the subject of David as if you're afraid that. . .that I'm still desperately in love with him, and the next you calmly chauffeur me to a formal dinner for two hundred people with David himself as host and expect me to feel as relaxed as I would with ten people at an office lunch. Is it any wonder I'm on edge? I'm——'

'Hey! Hey!' He reached out to her, his voice low and calm and his hand soft against the loose waves of her hair and the bare warm column of her neck.

They stared at each other in the darkness for a long moment, then he pulled her close to him and kissed her, a long satisfying kiss that drowned all doubts and questions—temporarily at least. His lips tasted fresh and felt firm, and he seemed to know instinctively exactly where to touch her in order to thrill every nerve-ending in her skin and send pulses through her that found the secret places in her body and made them tingle with need and longing.

Her fingers threaded themselves through his thick, clean hair, and the hardness of his muscles closing around her only made her own body feel softer and more fragile in its awareness. His lips traced a fiery line down her throat till they reached the swelling hint of her breasts at her beaded neckline and she knew an overpowering desire to slip the bodice from her shoulders so that his exploration of her throbbing curves could continue more freely. His hands were warm and hard through the thin silk fabric of her dress, reminding her that she wore little beneath it but lacy underwear, and it was only the sweeping beam of headlights from another car that put an end to the moment of reconciliation and rediscovery.

'Will that do for an apology?' he murmured as he slowly released her.

She drew a shuddering breath as their swelling of mutual desire slowly ebbed, then managed, 'An apology? For what?'

'You were right. I was insensitive. It seems that this is hard for both of us. . . Harder than I thought it would be.'

He frowned and turned away to reach for the door-handle, and by the time she had gathered her black beaded evening-bag he was beside her at the passenger door, holding it open. She couldn't question him about that last comment. Now was definitely not the time. With other sets of headlights sweeping across the gravel as two more cars turned to park in the large curved space to the east of the house, and the noise of music and conversation spilling from the open doors and windows, it had to be Juliet's public face that she showed for the next few hours.

'Ready?' Hugh murmured, taking her arm and guiding her across the smoothly raked white gravel.

He made a perfect escort for this sort of evening, Juliet thought, with a sudden inrush of that frighteningly giddy-making warmth about him that came increasingly often now. He did not need to be told, for example, that the ridiculous heels on these expensive black beaded evening shoes made walking on the loosely gravelled driveway next to impossible, and his hold on her arm was firm and steady, bringing an instant echo of the powerful sensations he had aroused in her moments ago in the car.

'Thank you,' she murmured with relief when they reached the firmer footing of the veranda.

'I'm glad you're not such a slave to fashions in footwear at work,' he answered with a teasing twist to his lips, as he released his caressing hold on her.

'So am I!' she breathed fervently, and they entered the spacious entrance hall on a note of shared laughter.

David Beckhill was there, and Juliet heard her laughter die away a little too abruptly as he strode forward. 'Hugh! At last!' he exclaimed, reaching out to pump his cousin's hand. 'I've been expecting you for the last half-hour. What happened?'

'Nothing, David,' Hugh answered, smoothly reassuring. 'Just another of the thousand and one unexpected events that happen in my game. I'm sorry we're late. How's it going so far?'

'Fine, fine,' David murmured nervously, looking past Hugh at some new arrivals coming up the wide stone steps. 'I wish to high heaven Dad hadn't insisted on launching the new wine this way, that's all. Hello, Juliet. . . Excuse me, this is Peter Mayhew from the *Herald*. He's just flown back from some extravagant, celebrity-studded junket in Paris, apparently, so I can just imagine what he'll say in his column next week if he doesn't like the wine. Snide comments about antipodean taste. . .'

He stepped past them to greet the influential food and wine writer and his equally influential architect wife. Again, Hugh guided Juliet calmly and expertly on into the crowded reception room, where hired staff glided about with trays of drinks and platters of delicate hors-d'oeuvres.

'David's very nervous,' Hugh said unnecessarily, as he secured a waiter's attention.

'Just tomato juice, please,' Juliet put in quickly, and he took two of them, handing her one cold, beaded glass and keeping the second for himself. Ice clinked at the rim and a garnish of lemon and mint added a fresh tang.

'Yes, he is nervous,' she added when the waiter had left them again. 'I gather he's launching a new wine tonight.'

'Yes. Uncle Lloyd's idea—the launch, that is, not the wine,' Hugh explained. 'David's been working for several years on introducing some of new grape varieties developed in California, which produce very light, fresh wines, and they're just bottled a white Zinfandel. Lloyd didn't want to have a Beckhill Zinfandel at all, but David really wanted to try it. It's the first project he's tackled fully on his own initiative and I'm afraid Uncle Lloyd didn't enjoy letting go of the reins. The launch. . .well, I shouldn't say it, perhaps, but, to be blunt, this launch is a petty revenge on his part. David wanted to introduce the wine quietly. It's quite a modest brew, by no means designed to be the 1990s' answer to champagne, but Lloyd insisted on spotlighting it like this, and David's afraid the whole thing will go down like a lead balloon.'

'And will it?' Juliet asked.

She found that her heart was thumping nervously and she dreaded the idea that David's innovation might fall flat on its face. Her professional knowledge of his and Alicia's infertility problem gave her extra compassion for him and she couldn't help wondering if Lloyd Beckhill knew about his son's heart-breaking difficulty in conceiving a child. It was the kind of thing many couples chose to keep very private.

'I don't know.' Hugh answered her question heavily, his eyes searching into her face as if the answer might be found there. 'This business is so dependent on fashion. I don't like Peter Mayhew and a couple of others of his ilk. They enjoy exercising power in their own very limited sphere, and the fact that they can destroy a restaurant or badly damage a winery's reputation with a few columns of clever insults disguised as healthy criticism seems to make them feel important. Not all of them are like that, of course, and a lot of the other people here will enjoy glamour of the evening and, we hope, promote the wine wonderfully in all sorts of ways as a result. Uncle Lloyd and my aunt Barbara are good at glamour, too. Look, there's a rather well-known actress on the arm of an even better known sportsman.' He pointed at a bright blonde head beside a pair of very beefy shoulders on the far side of the room. 'Some of the big wine retailers here tonight will very much enjoy meeting them, for example. . . So, will it fall flat? Only if David lets everyone see how tense he is.'

Juliet nodded silently. Following his gesture towards the actress and sportsman, she had seen them greet Alicia, and had seen, even from this distance, Alicia's white, strained face, which even heavy make-up could not disguise. If David was tense, then his wife looked stretched to breaking-point.

Then Alicia caught sight of Juliet and frowned, dampening the latter's initial reaction, which was to give a friendly wave. Then, while Juliet's hand was still poised uncertainly in the middle of the gesture, Alicia saw Hugh at her side and her frown disappeared, to be replaced by a curious and rather pleased smile. She returned Juliet's wave, then someone tapped her on the shoulder and she turned away, her face immediately resuming its strained expression.

What did all that mean? Juliet wondered inwardly. She was pleased to find that I was here with Hugh. Before that. . . Did she think David had invited me on my own? She couldn't be concerned about David and me, could she? *Jealous*. . .?

The thought filled her with dismay.

'. . .somewhere with our names on them.'

'I'm sorry,' Juliet blurted. 'I didn't hear what you said, Hugh.'

'I know,' he drawled. 'You were miles away. I said, people are starting to go in to dinner, so perhaps we should go and find our place. At this sort of affair you don't just plonk down next to someone with an interesting face.'

'No, I know. I expect David's been sweating over the seating arrangements for days.' Again, she spoke a little absently as she watched David and Alicia come together with a few terse words to each other. Neither of them looked assured by the other's presence.

'Actually, seating is usually Alicia's job, I think, and I'm sure that as usual she has done it very well, since it's something that helps and supports David,' Hugh answered very smoothly, and something in his tone made Juliet jerk her gaze upward to meet his thoughtful and slightly narrowed hazel eyes.

Why was he looking at her like that? It was disconcerting and not completely pleasant to be so thoroughly studied, and to her dismay she found herself blushing as she gabbled, 'Alicia's job, is it? Oh, all right, I didn't know. Well, I'm sure she *has* done it very well, yes.'

'Just as long as we're sitting together,' he said, still in an odd way, so that again her reply was awkward and self-conscious.

'Of course. They wouldn't separate us, would they, when I know almost no one here?'

As if fate was determined to embarrass her every time she spoke tonight, one of the few people she *did* know, Lloyd Beckhill, loomed before them at that moment.

'Hugh!' he said. 'Glad you could make it. You tasted the wine last week, didn't you?'

'Yes, David brought a bottle over to my place one evening, hot off the press, as it were, and a sample of the Grenache as well.'

'Yes, that's not ready for bottling yet. But what did you think of the Zinfandel?'

'Excellent, actually. A really good summer wine——'

'*Summer* wine. Exactly!' Lloyd growled ominously, his imposing silhouette, topped by thick grey-white hair, seeming to rise even higher as he spoke.

'But I mean that in the best sense,' Hugh parried coolly. 'In Australia, summer wine is what people want—fresh, cool and glowing, for evening barbecues and beach picnics.'

'Hmph!' Lloyd Beckhill snorted dismissively, but Juliet could see that Hugh's steady confidence had discomfited his rather formidable uncle, and she wondered whether it was Hugh's skill and success in the utterly unrelated field of medicine that gave him the courage and certainty that David lacked in dealing with his father.

But Lloyd Beckhill was speaking again. 'And now . . .who's this?' he enquired genially.

'Juliet Rohan,' Hugh said briefly.

Juliet smiled and put out a hand in greeting, about to create some polite piece of chat about meeting again after so long, but then, as she met the senior Beckhill's intelligent light brown eyes, she realised with a cold shock that he. . . No, he *did* recognise her! He knew exactly who she was and how she fitted into his son's past, and yet he was deliberately pretending—in a genial, fatherly sort of way—that she was some sweet young thing of Hugh's whom he had never met before in his life.

The little game had the desired effect, what was more. She grew hot and uncomfortable at once, and the few words she managed to produce made little sense. She felt Hugh's grip tighten on her arm and then heard with relief his, 'You're busy, Uncle Lloyd. Perhaps we'll have time to talk later.'

Neither she nor Hugh mentioned the exchange, but he kept up a steady stream of easy conversation as they searched for and found their place settings at one of the twenty long tables, and she thought that he had to be the most considerate and sensitive man she had ever met, sensing her embarrassment like that and doing his best to put her at her ease.

Gradually, the other diners took their places and the meal began. It was designed to highlight a range of Beckhill wines, with the new white Zinfandel to be served with dessert before the gathering became less formal again with a buffet cheese course.

Seated next to Hugh and Juliet were several important people in the world of wine, and she realised how difficult it must have been for Hugh to break away from the family tradition by going into medicine. Clearly, Lloyd Beckhill could easily have found a strong role for his nephew in promoting the company, and there was still the subtle but very strong expectation that he would take a high profile at gatherings such as this one.

Juliet was content to remain quiet as she savoured

the cream of carrot soup followed by beef Wellington and a delicious selection of fresh spring vegetables. David and Alicia sat at the next table, at the centre of the proceedings, and Juliet could see that the eight people who shared the table with them were the cream—in terms of importance—of the crop of guests this evening. Alicia had a stiff, too-brilliant smile set on her face as she nodded at Peter Mayhew's pedantic tirade, while David seemed to be telling a joke or two—and telling them badly, if the response from the other guests was any indication. He was only picking at his food, too.

The noise level in the large room rose and Juliet began to feel claustrophobic in her glittering dress. If Dad hadn't lost his business that might be me, now, next to David, she thought. While Hugh would be here with someone else. I'd hate it. I'd hate to live this life all the time.

With a sudden surge of panic, she knew she had to get away to cool down a little before the main course was cleared away and David's moment in the spotlight came. Leaving the last mouthfuls of the succulent beef in its pastry crust, she murmured an excuse to Hugh and rose, swishing the silk of her dress to one side as she brushed past his strong torso.

He broke off his conversation with the man opposite and turned to her to say in a rapid undertone, 'You all right? You look pale. . .'

'I'm fine. Back in a minute,' she answered, and hurried away before he could notice the dew of perspiration on her bare collarbone.

Conjuring her past visits to this house with difficulty, she remembered that there was a very private bathroom tucked away behind the formal staircase that led to the upper floors, and after one wrong turning she found it and saw thankfully that it was empty. Most of the guests would be directed to the larger men's and ladies' rooms beyond the end of the entrance hall, so with any luck she would have this powder-blue and gold haven to herself.

It was very quiet in here. At first she simply stood in front of the vanity basin staring unseeingly into the mirror, aware of the faint hum that was the roar of conversation in the dining hall and the more abrupt sounds of crashing cutlery and rushing taps that came from the huge kitchen out the back. Then, realising that her time was far from infinite, she splashed her wrists with cold water and dappled a few droplets on neck and face, not daring to do more in case she smudged the make-up that she had applied more heavily than usual this evening.

Hugh had said she looked pale, but now her cheeks were flushed and her blue eyes too dominant with their long lashes blackened by mascara and her lids tinted with silvery gold eye-shadow. Only her lips looked bare of colour, since her lipstick had disappeared as she ate, so she took the coral-toned tube out of her small evening-bag and re-applied it carefully, hoping that it was only the bright lights surrounding the mirror that brought out the colour tones so strongly.

I look too much like that actress, she thought. My room is too dark at home to put all this on properly.

Then, realising that this sort of self-criticism was not helping to calm her down, she left the haven of the brightly lit room. . .and came face to face with David.

'Oh, Juliet, thank God you're here!' he breathed shakily, and she realised that he had fled the dining hall, as she had done, to gain some courage alone.

She was about to step aside so that he could enter the bathroom, searching in her mind at the same time

for some friendly words of reassurance, but then she
saw the real suffering in his eyes and in a moment of
compassion and tenderness she laid a hand on his arm
and said, 'You can do it, David. The evening is
marvellous already, and the only people who aren't
looking forward to the wine are the people who are so
weary and blasé about life that they wouldn't look
forward to having afternoon tea with. . .with Henry
the Eighth and his six wives.'

He laughed briefly, but could not fully be distracted
by her attempt at humour. 'Really, though?' he said.
'You're enjoying yourself?'

'Of course I am. Our table is talking its head off and
everyone has cleaned their plates. That Cabernet
Merlot you chose to go with the beef Wellington was
delicious. You *know* you can do this, David.'

She smiled up at him, her hand still resting on his
arm as she stroked her fingers lightly across the firmly
woven black wool of his dinner jacket. With a new
kindly of affection for him, she was about to brush her
lips against his cheek, and then move on down the
passage, when suddenly he lunged at her, enfolding
her in a tight, hungry embrace that left her almost
winded and utterly unable to break free as she immediately wanted to do.

'Damn it, Juliet, if only things were different!' he
was saying hotly into the thick, glossy fall of her hair,
and then he was kissing her feverishly, or trying to,
seeming unaware that her own mouth had not
responded and that she was now speaking to him,
urging him to let her go.

'David, please!'

The worst thing about it was that she understood
everything he was feeling and still ached with sympathy
for him. Lloyd Beckhill had been cruel to insist on this

evening, and life was cruel, too, at the moment, with Alicia's false hope and disappointment repeating its tragic pattern every month like a travesty of nature's rhythm, taking its toll on their marriage and David's deepest sense of worth.

'David, let me go. This isn't right.'

His lips, hot and demanding, brought memory flooding back of a time when these same lips had been laughing and coaxing, and when she had willingly returned his kisses. In a final moment of tenderness, she let her arms hold him, and although she tried to turn her face away from his kiss so that their contact was like that between a brother and sister, she couldn't succeed at once and her words were still being spoken against the desperate pressure of his mouth.

'I know how hard it is for you, and for Alicia——'

And at last, at that moment, he let her go.

'Your father sent me to look for you, David.' Hugh's voice cutting like an icy blade in the warm air made Juliet spin around at once with a whipping swirl of her silk dress. It had been the sight of him, rounding the corner in the passage on the thick, silent carpeting, that had caused David to release her, not her own entreaties to him.

There was a silence after Hugh's remark and Juliet could see that David was struggling to master himself. In only a few seconds, he did so, and now looked more in control and more defiantly sure of himself than he had done all evening.

'Right,' he said. 'They're ready for my introduction, are they?'

'Yes, the main course has been cleared away. Alicia wondered what had happened to you.' David didn't answer. He was already striding along the corridor, leaving Hugh and Juliet behind. 'We'd better get back too,' Hugh continued heavily.

'Yes.' She searched for a way to explain what he had seen and realised sickeningly that there wasn't one.

Any excuse would sound. . .just like that: an excuse, an attempt to justify something that simply wasn't justifiable. If Hugh trusted her enough to wait until a time later on when they were alone together and could talk about what had happened in a reasonable way, then things might be all right. If he *didn't* trust her enough. . .

But that possibility was too painful to contemplate.

A minute later, they arrived back in the dining hall and took their places at the table, still in silence.

'Marvellous, Lloyd, really marvellous,' Peter Mayhew said, pumping his host's hand vigorously. 'Beckhill Estates has done it again. I tell you frankly that I came here ready to scoff, but David is right. It's a delightful wine. Unpretentious, not trying to set the world on fire, but on the right occasion. . .perfect. I wouldn't like to see Beckhill's abandon its tried and true wines— the heavy reds that you do so well——'

'Abandon the reds? Never!' Lloyd agreed strongly.

'But it's good to see the diversity you've established with these new light varieties. You must be very proud of David.'

'Very proud. He's learnt a lot from me over the past few years.' Lloyd clamped a hearty hand on his son's shoulder and shook it manfully.

David grinned and began an anecdote with a flourish that contrasted utterly with his nervous, off-key performance three hours ago. He did not seem to bear any grudge towards his father, but Juliet seethed inwardly. Lloyd Beckhill had done as much as he could to undermine his son's sense of self-worth and ability tonight, but now that David had won through Lloyd was more than happy to bask in the glory. The man's ego and arrogance, which at seventeen she had been too immature to recognise, went a long way towards explaining the weaknesses she now saw so clearly in David—weaknesses which Hugh did not seem to share.

'Come on,' he said in her ear. 'We don't need to make a fuss about saying goodbye. If we can squeeze past this bottleneck no one will even notice we've gone.'

'Yes, I'd prefer that,' Juliet said carefully, and a few minutes later they were free of the enthusiastic crowds clustered around David and his father, and out in the now-chilly late August night air.

David had made a wonderful performance of introducing the wine. His speech had been interesting and witty, and just the right length, and he had selected fresh berry soufflés for dessert—a choice that brought out all the freshness that was the new wine's main strength. Juliet's own performance had been excellent as well. No one would have suspected her tension and misery as she exclaimed over the dessert and wine, and made animated conversation over cheese, coffee, liqueurs and chocolates.

Between the final courses, a band had struck up and she had danced with Hugh and other partners like Hans Andersen's little mermaid, so light on her feet, with the beading on her dress sparkling as she whirled beneath the chandeliers, that no one would ever guess that her heart was breaking. . .and that her shoes pinched and blistered her feet like blunt knife blades.

Now, as she walked to the car beside Hugh, she cherished one faint remaining hope that being alone with him would make things all right again, but when they had reached the low-slung Jaguar without a word passing between them she knew that her hope was in vain.

And she could scarcely blame him. If I had rounded a corner and come upon him and Alicia locked together like that, what would I have thought? she asked herself, and the answer was very simple. She would have been as angry and unforgiving as Hugh so clearly was now. She couldn't help searching and searching for a way to explain, wanted to blurt out an apology, an admission of guilt, anything. . .but the words would not come, and finally, as they rolled down the driveway, gravel crunching and popping beneath the tyres, she fully realised why.

She felt so much to blame for what had happened. Her sympathy for David had been too ready and too warm, coming from a woman who had once been engaged to him. And as a professional who was aware of his fertility problem, and aware, too, of how that could affect any man's self-esteem, she should have kept a more deliberate distance. Why had she not done so? Could it be that there was more feeling left in her for David than she had ever admitted to herself? Those times when Hugh had treated the subject like walking on eggshells. . . Had he understood more clearly than she herself what was going on inside her?

Only the dying sound of Hugh's car engine pulled her from the downward-spiralling thoughts, and when she focused her gaze she realised that they were already parked outside her front gate. There was an uncomfortable silence now that the throaty purr of the engine was gone, then, while she still searched for a way to say thank you and goodnight, Hugh spoke.

'This evening has been a mess,' he said.

'Yes, I'm——' she began, but he cut her off abruptly.

'Look, I don't know what your involvement is with David, but——'

'There isn't an involvement,' she blurted desperately. 'What you saw was. . .was nothing. David was upset and nervous and——'

'Please, Juliet. I don't want to hear this. A moment of passion, a fully fledged affair——'

'Not that, Hugh! For heaven's sake, what sort of a person do you think I am?'

'All right,' he conceded on a sigh. 'Perhaps it was just a kiss for old times' sake. I'm trying to say, though, that it makes no difference. Somehow, for one of you or for both of you, there's still something left over from what happened between you years ago. . .' He paused for a tiny beat as if waiting for her to rush to deny his words, but, with her own doubts about what she still felt for David, she couldn't say anything at all, and a second later he continued, 'I've. . .been afraid all along that that was the case and as far as I'm concerned that makes things impossible. For you and me, I mean.'

'Yes, I understand,' she murmured, but so softly that he might not have heard.

'I might as well be honest about it,' he went on, his tone cool and firm, every word clearly and confidently spoken. 'I've. . .very much enjoyed the time we've spent together, but it broke two of my cardinal rules. I tried to forget that we were professional colleagues, and, more importantly, I tried to forget that you'd once been engaged to my cousin, but I think tonight has made it clear that we both would have done better to have remembered those things and steered clear of this from the beginning. I don't think we should see each other again.'

'See each other?' she echoed on a laugh that almost succeeded in masking the pain she felt. 'We'll be seeing each other every day.'

'I know. . .but you know what I meant. And if you felt that you wanted to leave the practice I'd make sure there was no problem about references and that kind of thing.'

'But I *don't* want to leave!' she exclaimed. 'I can't. I. . .I like it here,' she finished lamely, wondering if that could be the truth now that this terrible thing had happened with Hugh.

'Do you? I'm glad,' he said, and she was very relieved that the dark country night hid her expression from him. 'I enjoy working with you very much.'

'Yes, it's a nice practice,' she agreed, scarcely caring what nonsense she spoke now. 'But I mustn't keep you sitting here. It's very late. Thank you for the evening. I'm sorry it hasn't worked out. I——' She broke off.

'Yes?'

'Nothing. Thank you again, Hugh. Goodnight.'

'Goodnight, Juliet.'

Carefully, she stepped from the car and closed the door behind her. Steadily, she walked up the path and let herself in, to be greeted by the warm, wraith-like shape of Spats rubbing himself against the silky froth of fabric around her ankles. Tiredly, she poured a saucer of milk for him, waited until he had lapped it clean then held the back door open as he left the cottage in search of nocturnal adventure. Then she climbed the stairs, unfastened the beaded silk dress and let it fall carelessly to the floor, lay across the bed in her lacy underwear and cried for a long time.

CHAPTER SIX

'AND now Juliet will go round to each couple and help you practice the breathing technique while I set up tonight's video and put on the kettle for tea and coffee,' Margaret Chatham said.

It was a Thursday night, six days after that memorable wine launch at the Beckhill estate, and Juliet was assisting at her first childbirth class. Over the past two weeks, she had spent two evenings at Margaret's, where the classes were held, going over the course material and making sure that she herself was familiar with all the breathing and relaxation techniques that Margaret taught.

Now, ten couples sat on comfortable cushions in the carpeted recreation room at the Chathams', and they had just been taught the first of several breathing patterns which would be used at different stages throughout labour and delivery. Juliet had passed around information sheets, demonstrated the first breathing pattern while Margaret explained it, and had spent the rest of this first night trying to commit everyone's names to memory as Margaret talked about the course and the ideas that lay behind the goal of natural childbirth.

'Just continue to practise on your own, everyone,' she said now as she took over the central teaching role. 'I'll spend time with each couple, using the stop-watch to see if you're breathing at the right rate, and please ask questions, too, if you have any.'

She spent fifteen minutes going round the room and

found that most couples were having no trouble with the technique, and that most questions related to things that would be coming up later in the course, which took place over four evenings. It was only the last couple who seemed sceptical about the idea of natural childbirth.

'But if I'm in horrible pain right from the beginning. . .' blonde, spiky-haired, twenty-one-year-old Robyn said as the group began to break up into informal knots of conversation. Some people headed for the kitchen where tea, coffee, juice and biscuits were now waiting, and one or two drifted up to listen to Robyn. 'I just can't see that I'll care about breathing,' she went on. 'I'll want something to wipe out the pain straight away. I mean, if possible I'd just like to wake up and discover I've got a beautiful baby and it's all over. I know I'm not supposed to feel like that, I'm supposed to think it's going to be the most wonderful experience of my whole life, but I don't. I'm scared of it, and I don't see why doctors can't make it easy and pain-free.'

'Gosh!' Juliet said with a smile, although she did feel a little burdened by the speech, since she couldn't give the easy answers that Robyn was looking for. Suppressing a sigh, she continued, 'I'm afraid what you're asking is to have your cake and eat it too. There's really no way to guarantee a pain-free childbirth, although some people are lucky enough to have a short labour that's only mildly uncomfortable. The only way to guarantee painless labour is to do a scheduled Caesarean under general anaesthetic——'

'It sounds marvellous!' Robyn said frankly.

'I said painless *labour*,' Juliet pointed out. 'After the birth is another story. Don't forget that it's major abdominal surgery.'

'That's right,' put in one of the other women, Judy. 'My sister-in-law couldn't sit up without help for a week, and her scar still itched like crazy months later.'

'Tea's ready, everyone,' Margaret said in the doorway. 'What's the delay?'

Juliet is telling us that we can't have our cake and eat it too,' Judy's husband Mike said with a grin. He seemed nice, Juliet thought—supportive of his wife and interested in the course.

'I don't want to suffer,' Robyn explained. 'And Juliet says I'll have to. I loathe pain and I'll probably faint at the first contraction and die.'

'You've been watching too many melodromatic films,' Margaret admonished, and everyone laughed. 'Wait till the course is finished and see how you feel then.'

'My due date will be three weeks closer then, so I'll probably feel much worse,' Robyn said with exaggerated gloom. Everyone laughed again and the issue was defused—for the moment, at least.

'When you've all got your drinks, come through into the living-room and we'll watch the video,' Margaret announced. 'It will show you some examples of normal labour and delivery, and was filmed in Adelaide a few years ago. You might even recognise someone in it!'

Juliet hadn't seen the video herself, so she settled down with tea and a cream biscuit, prepared to enjoy the passive role of sitting here in the dim light taking in the images on the screen. The thirty-minute video was well-presented, and should go some way towards lessening Robyn's exaggerated fears, Juliet thought. Three couples were featured, each with a different story, although all three births fell into the normal range, and all were drug-free.

It was only in the last few minutes of the video that

the camera focused on the face of one of the doctors doing a delivery, and with a shock of recognition Juliet saw that it was Hugh. She glanced at Margaret straight away and saw the older woman's amused smile, just as several other people in the room gave surprised exclamations, and Judy Minster said, 'But that's Dr Beckhill! He looks quite a bit younger.'

'I'll tell him my childbirth class thinks he's aged badly,' Margaret teased, and Judy was horrified.

'Don't you dare! I didn't mean it like that,' she said.

Meanwhile, Juliet could only stare at the moving images on the screen—Hugh's serious face, his gloved hands as he eased the slippery vernix-covered baby out. He *did* look younger, but she thought he was far better looking now that professional experience and confidence had firmed in his features. It shouldn't be so painful to see him like this. After all, she had seen him at work all this week, but somehow here in the dimly lit room, where she did not have to force herself to play the role of competent nurse for the moment, the deep well of hurt and disappointment that she had been repressing since that abandonment of tears on Friday night came flooding to the surface.

There had been so much promise behind the rapid growth of their involvement, and it had felt so easy and right to let herself be washed with the tide of feelings that Hugh's presence seemed to produce in her without effort. Then she thought back more searchingly to those few golden times they had spent together and realised that, after all, it had been not quite as perfect and rosy as she was now thinking. Even then there had been hints of trouble, moments of doubt in both of them. But while she had been rapidly overcoming her doubts, laying the ghost of her past with David, Hugh's doubts, it seemed, had only been growing.

His face came on to the screen again, smiling his congratulations at the couple who were now immersed in greeting their new baby, and Juliet thought about how he had smiled at her on several occasions this week. It would have been easier, she decided, if he hadn't.

Yes, she would have preferred him to be distant and taciturn, but instead he remained friendly, courteous, considerate, and that only made her the more miserable that the brief spark between them had been quenched into nothingness.

The video ended and Margaret brightened the lights again while she rewound the tape. 'Any questions?' she said as she collected cups and saucers on a tray to return them to the kitchen.

'Do those tennis balls really help?' a dark, petite woman named Ellen said sceptically.

'Yes, they do,' Margaret answered. 'I know it looks odd, seeing the husband pressing tennis balls in a sock into his wife's lower back, but if the baby's head is pressing back against the spinal column then strong counter-pressure can really ease that, and the tennis balls are the right shape and firmness to get right in there to the exact spot. In a minute, I'll give you a sheet of suggested things to bring to the labour-room, and we'll go through it in case anything else on it strikes you as odd, like those tennis balls.'

Most faces nodded brightly at this, but Juliet, able to observe more carefully than Margaret could while she was talking, noticed that again Robyn and her husband looked sceptical and unhappy. They were both quiet for the rest of the class and Juliet jotted down a memo to herself in her diary to check when Robyn's next office visit was scheduled. The nervous mother-to-be usually saw Hugh, and perhaps he could put in an encouraging word. Not many couples dropped out of the classes, but Robyn and her husband might easily do so. Hugh could give a more official seal of approval to the methods that Margaret promoted, and it might be enough to kindle Robyn's interest a little further.

Juliet came across the memo the next morning as she snatched a moment at ten o'clock to make a quick cup of coffee. The office was busy and all three doctors had patients, but for five minutes she had no one to weigh and no tests to run so, coffee in hand, she borrowed the appointment book from Debbie and flipped through it till she found Robyn's name: next Friday at eleven. That was a pity. It would be too late to give her a pep talk before next Thursday's class. She returned the appointment book to Debbie, who needed it again.

The phone rang, and Debbie said, 'Can you get it, Juliet?'

'Surely.' She picked it up without a second thought and said an automatic, 'Dr Gordon and Associates.'

'Juliet?'

'Yes, speaking. Who is this, please?' Although she knew quite well already. It was David Beckhill.

'I've been wanting to talk to you for days,' he said. 'Is there some time I can come round? To the surgery or to your place, I don't mind.'

'I don't think that's a good idea, Dav——' she answered carefully, biting off the last half of his name.

She was very aware of Debbie Miller beside her, as well as Anne Thomas on the other side of the desk, consulting with the secretary about her next appointment. Red-haired Anne and her husband Rick ran a very successful hotel and restaurant here in Romney-vale and knew David and Alicia Beckhill quite well. In fact, they had also been guests at last Friday's launch, although Juliet wasn't sure if they had noticed her own presence there.

'Listen,' David was saying, 'we need to talk. I won't be fobbed off.'

'Can you hold the line for a moment while I switch to another phone?' she answered as blandly and lightly as she could.

'Of course, yes; you're not alone, are you?' he said.

'No, and the waiting-room's full. I only have a minute. Literally.'

'OK, my timing was bad. Sorry.'

'Wait a moment and I'll switch the phone. . . Debbie, I'm going to pick up in the testing-room. Can you switch it there in half a minute when I've got there?' she said quickly.

'OK.' Debbie looked up from the appointment card she was writing for Anne Thomas, and Juliet hurried to the relative privacy of the testing-room.

She didn't shut the door, since Margaret came in and out of there regularly and any of the three doctors might poke their heads in with a question, an instruction, or a request for some equipment, but as far as privacy went it was the best she was going to get.

With a sigh and a sense of foreboding, she picked up the phone. 'Hello, David, are you still there?'

'Yes, I am. Look, Juliet, it's very simple and it won't take long. I want to apologise for the other night. There's no excuse. I was nervous about the launch, and, as you know, things haven't been easy between me and Alicia lately. But I shouldn't have embroiled you. I let myself wonder if things would be better for me now if I had stuck to my guns and married you——'

'Don't, David,' she interrupted desperately, staring

unseeingly at the desk in front of her. 'Don't let's even think about those might-have-beens. I have no regrets.'

A noise in the doorway made her look up and she saw Vern Gordon standing there. 'Get out a size seventy diaphragm for Mrs Allen, would you, Juliet?'

'Yes, Dr Gordon.'

And directly behind him was Hugh. 'Here's an alpha-fetoprotein test to get ready for the path lab,' he said in his turn, his eye on the phone receiver still pressed to her ear.

She nodded and took the blood vial from him, knowing from his face that he had heard part of her conversation and knew very well who was on the other end of the line. He left again at once, and she heard the door to the waiting-room open and his voice, steady and friendly, as he called in his next patient, whose weight, urine, and blood-pressure Margaret had just taken.

Once again, his departure meant that there was nothing to be said, and she almost thought she would have preferred it if he had slammed the door of the testing-room, shutting them in together so that he could unleash a verbal tirade upon her. Then, at least, she could have vented some of her own feelings in anger instead of having to wait with silent patience until they drained slowly and painfully away.

She was holding the receiver away from her ear now, and still had the blood vial—which had to be dealt with immediately—in her other hand. An intermittent buzzing voice told her that David was saying her name, wondering why there was no response. Slowly she brought the instrument close again and spoke.

'Sorry, David. I have to go. Thanks for your call. Your apology is accepted, but let's not refer to any of this again, all right?'

'Of course. I was going to suggest the same thing.
Bye, Juliet.'

He hung up, leaving her—perversely—with a sense
that their talk was unfinished, and she wondered unhap-
pily whether it would always be like this with David.
Perhaps her life had changed too abruptly nearly nine
years ago, and her emotions about their engagement
and its ending had not died, as she had thought, but had
only been hidden somewhere within her, to come out
only now when she didn't want them at all.

'There's one couple missing. Now, who is it? I'd better
check my list,' Margaret said at childbirth class the
following Thursday.

'It's Robyn and Jim,' Juliet put in. She wasn't
surprised at their absence, but had been checking for
their arrival as each new couple entered the room. In a
more confidential tone to Margaret she added, 'She
has an appointment tomorrow, and I'm going to ask
Hugh to put in a positive word about the classes.'

'Yes, she did seem rather half-hearted last week,'
Margaret agreed. 'An added recommendation from
Hugh might help. Good idea.'

Juliet didn't say that she had been planning to have
this word with Hugh for some days now and had been
putting it off. Their exchanges had been strictly practical and very, very brief on both sides this week, and
she found that there was a safety in this that she didn't
want to lose. She had been hoping that Margaret would
say, 'I'll speak to him about it,' but of course she
didn't, since it was the kind of routine communication
about a patient's feelings that passed between doctors
and nurses all the time.

The class proceeded uneventfully, and all the couples
worked hard, listening carefully to Margaret's expla-

nation of the active and transition phases of labour and practising the two new breathing techniques she taught them. Tonight's video dealt with breast-feeding, and then came a relaxation session which would give the expectant mothers and their husbands some ideas about how to stay calm in early labour. 'Since we don't want the traditional panicky dash to the hospital as soon as you feel the first contraction,' Margaret said.

'It really is a pity that Robyn and Jim missed this class,' she observed to Juliet as they packed up equipment later, after the class was over, 'since it's the meatiest of the lot.'

'They'll have to pick it up during revision in the last class,' Juliet said. 'That is, if we can persuade them to come back again at all.'

'Oh, Hugh's pretty clever at that sort of thing, I'm starting to realise,' the older nurse said confidently, as she bundled up the charts and diagrams she used and stored them away in a wall cupboard.

'Yes, he is, isn't he?' Juliet answered a little hollowly, and she didn't notice the sharp glance that Margaret gave in her direction.

Robyn Ellis arrived promptly for her appointment the next day. Juliet had talked to Hugh about her just half an hour before.

'I'll do what I can,' had been his response, delivered in the friendly yet subtly reserved way in which he always spoke to her now.

It was this that Juliet was thinking about as she did the urinalysis, noted down the weight gain and took Robyn into the examining-room to take her blood-pressure.

'I've been feeling a bit bloated over the last few days,' Robyn said as she held out her arm for the blood-pressure cuff.

'Have you?' Juliet answered a little absently. 'Yes, the weather has been unseasonably warm this week. My cottage garden is bursting into life, but I know it's hard if you're pregnant. You'd probably rather winter kept going until November this year.'

She pumped up the cuff, saw the result on the wall scale, and something finally clicked. What was that weight gain she had noted down? Without giving anything away by her expression, she went to Robyn's chart and noted down the blood-pressure reading, which was not dangerously high, but definitely higher than it should be.

She checked the weight gain and saw that it, too, was a little alarming. A gain of four kilograms in only two weeks, and Robyn had just complained of feeling swollen and bloated. The urinalysis had shown no sign of proteinuria. That, at least, couldn't have slipped past her, but the other two symptoms should definitely be brought to Hugh's attention.

He came in at that moment, and Robyn greeted him enthusiastically from the examining bench where she sat. 'Hi, Dr Beckhill. I like your shirt.'

'Thank you,' he smiled, touching the crisp grey fabric, faintly pin-striped in white, as if surprised that she had noticed it. Then he turned to Juliet with a questioning look, since she usually slipped out of the examining-room as soon as he arrived, and this time she hadn't done so.

She pointed to the chart entries she had made and he took in their significance straight away, nodding briefly. She left, noticing as she did so that Robyn's eyes never left the obstetrician's face, and that her cheeks had taken on a pretty pink flush.

She's got a little crush on him, Juliet realised with an odd pang. I suppose that's hardly surprising. . .

Encountering Robyn again ten minutes later as the heavily pregnant young woman stood at the front desk making her next appointment, Juliet said, 'Is everything all right?'

'Oh, yes,' Robyn answered confidently. 'Dr Beckhill explained it all. He said I'm showing a couple of warning signs for toxaemia, but there's nothing to worry about yet. I have to cut down on salt and have plenty of bed rest—today's my last day at work, so that should be easy enough—lying on my left side. He also said it's really important that I keep going to the birthing classes, so I know what to do and don't panic. If the toxaemia doesn't go away, I might have to have a Caesarean,' she finished happily, still clearly considering this the easiest and most attractive option. That the idea of toxaemia didn't worry her must be a tribute to Hugh Beckhill's professionally reassuring manner, Juliet decided.

'I gather you weren't too worried about Robyn Ellis's symptoms,' she forced herself to say a little later when bringing a patient's file to him as he waited on the phone to the hospital. It was hard to chat to him like this, but they couldn't go on meeting with painful silences and minimal exchanges, and it was up to her to meet his careful friendliness halfway.

'I wouldn't say "not worried",' he answered lightly. 'But I didn't want to worry *her*. Some women read everything they can on pregnancy and know that toxaemia can become a life-threatening condition, but with someone like Robyn, who clearly feels that ignorance is bliss, I only tell her what she needs to know. She's coming in again next Tuesday for another checkup and in the meantime she knows what symptoms I want to hear about straight away.'

'The risk is still low, isn't it, at this stage?'

'Yes,' he nodded, 'and with any luck that water retention and elevated blood-pressure will have gone again by Tuesday.'

'Thanks for weaving in the childbirth classes so successfully,' Juliet said. 'You can obviously wrap her around your little finger.'

'You think so?' he laughed. 'I'll wait until the delivery-room before I decide if you're right. Hang on.' He turned quickly to the phone receiver that had been waiting in his hand all this time. 'Yes, Dr Mitchell. No, don't send her home. I'd like to examine her myself. Until I get there, can you. . .?'

Juliet let herself out of the office and closed the door with a gentle click, trying to satisfy herself that the very ordinary and quite pleasant exchange meant that she was beginning to get her emotions under control where Hugh Beckhill was concerned. In time it might even be possible to forget that crazy, wonderful, disturbing set of feelings that had bubbled to the surface so easily a few weeks ago. . .

Robyn Ellis's toxaemia symptoms had subsided considerably by the following Tuesday, and she and her husband turned up to childbirth class two days later, outwardly willing if inwardly still somewhat sceptical. Then, on Wednesday six days later, Dr Gordon arrived at the surgery in the morning looking somewhat the worse for wear and yawning at regular intervals behind his hand.

'Busy night last night,' he said. 'And I delivered one of your patients at six o'clock this morning, Hugh,' he said to his third partner, who had not been on call last night.

'Really?' Hugh answered. 'I'll owe you an extra night soon at this rate. I haven't been called out since last Thursday. Who was it?'

'Robyn Ellis.' Then the senior obstetrician laughed. 'She had a three-hour labour, popped young Richard James out on the third push, and said it was so easy, less painful than menstrual cramps, she didn't need to bother with any fancy breathing and she didn't know what all the fuss was about!'

Juliet joined in the general laughter, but exchanged a speaking glance with Margaret as well. Both of them were aware of the irony.

'I only hope that now one of our enthusiastic, well-informed women like Judy or Elizabeth or Melanie doesn't go on and have a gruelling labour with complications!' the older nurse said to Juliet in an undertone.

'Yes,' the latter agreed. 'That would add insult to injury, wouldn't it?'

'But listen to us!' Margaret went on. 'It sounds as if we were wishing a long labour on Robyn out of spite because she didn't take our classes seriously.'

'Well, we *do* like to be appreciated, let's face it!' Juliet answered. Both women laughed again, then set about the business of the day, after Margaret had refused to tell Hugh the cause of their amusement.

The last class of the September childbirth course took place the next day, although a new lot of couples would assemble the following week—a smaller group that Juliet would run alone as Margaret was going on holiday. Robyn Ellis was the only one of the ten women to have delivered so far, and she had been about ten days early, but the other due dates were fast approaching, with Judy due next Tuesday and Melanie lamenting the fact that she would probably be the last in about five weeks' time.

Everyone was eager to hear from Margaret and Juliet about Robyn's experience and all the women hoped for as easy a time as she had had.

'Three hours' labour, did you say?' Elizabeth queried. She was a serious but likeable woman of thirty-four, an accountant by profession, and overjoyed at her impending motherhood after a long wait.

'Yes, that's what Dr Gordon told us,' Juliet answered.

'And you've said that the average first labour is twelve hours.'

'That's right.'

'So that means the rest of us will have to go. . .' she pretended to be adding up figures on a pocket calculator '. . .an hour longer each, to keep it statistically correct. Oh, no!'

There was a burst of laughter and then the class got down to the serious business of revising everything they had learnt, ranging from breathing techniques during second-stage labour to where the husbands should park their cars in the hospital car park.

'Feeling all right?' Juliet asked Judy when the class was almost over.

She was going round to each couple on the right side of the room listening to their breathing one final time, while Margaret listened to those on the left side. Judy had broken off her steady rhythm and then resumed it with a look of concentration that suggested she really was in pain.

'I'm fine,' Judy nodded. 'Just some Braxton-Hicks contractions. I've been having a lot of them over the past few days and they're getting quite painful.'

'It sounds as if your baby might not wait till Tuesday.'

'That's fine by me. The sooner, the better!' Like most women, she was anxious for the uncomfortable weeks of late pregnancy to be over and done with.

Ten minutes later, the class ended with good wishes

all round, and promises to keep in touch. People began
to gather bags and jackets, and as Judy bent down to
collect her own leather-strapped shoulder-bag there
was a splashing sound and a cry of surprise and dismay
from her. 'My waters have broken! Oh, Margaret, your
carpet!'

'Don't be silly, Judy, it really is just like water. It
won't stain. Everyone, this seems pretty dramatic,
doesn't it, but can I ask you not to hang around?' And
then, as Judy tightened her body against the evident
onslaught of pain, 'We'll call Dr Steinbeck and see
what he has to say, but there's nothing for the rest of
you to do. I think you're in labour, Judy.'

The other eight couples filed out, their end-of-class
high spirits rather toned down by this new turn of
events, while Judy's husband Mike held his wife's
shoulders to try to keep her calm and to hide his own
nervousness.

'How long is it since that pain you thought was a
Braxton-Hicks?' Juliet asked, while Margaret went into
the living-room to ring the practice's answering service,
who would put her immediately in touch with Geoffrey
Steinbeck. She looked at her watch. 'Must be about
ten minutes.'

'Yes, but I had another one about five minutes ago,'
Judy confessed. 'I didn't say anything about it because
I still didn't think it meant anything.' She was shaking
slightly now, unprepared for going into labour in such
a dramatic way. 'Shall I start the breathing?' she
wanted to know.

'Not yet,' Juliet advised. 'Save it for a little later on.
For the moment just rest, or walk around if you'd
rather do that.'

'Walk around.' Judy nodded. 'All right.' And she
and Mike started circling the room slowly together.

Less than five minutes later, another and significantly stronger pain gripped her, and she cried out.

'Try and keep calm,' Juliet said, but Judy's voice drowned out her reassuring words.

'No, something's wrong. I can feel it. It doesn't feel right.'

'How? What do you mean?'

Margaret re-entered at that moment. 'Dr Steinbeck is already at the hospital,' she said. 'He wants us to examine you here and call him back. He expects to be in the delivery-room in about half an hour, so——' She broke off as she saw Judy's panic-stricken face. 'What is it?'

'I can feel something pushing out. That shouldn't be happening, should it? Is it the baby? It doesn't feel right.'

'Get down on all fours,' Margaret said. 'Juliet. . .'

But Juliet had already gone to the bathroom to wash her hands thoroughly and fetch several clean towels. She returned in a few moments and said, 'I'll examine her in that position. If it is what you suspect, Margaret. . .'

The older woman nodded briefly and Juliet wasted no more time, using the towels both for Judy to kneel on and to protect her privacy a little as the awkward examination took place. Juliet was quick to reach a verdict.

'Yes,' she said as she rose and took the towel that Margaret handed her. 'The cord is starting to prolapse. The baby's head still isn't engaged, and——'

'That's serious, isn't it?' Judy interrupted. Her calm tone masked a well of fear.

'It can be,' Juliet answered carefully.

Margaret had already left the room to return to the telephone. An ambulance was needed now, and who-

ever was second on call, since Dr Steinbeck, with
another delivery imminent, could not perform the
emergency Caesarean that would now be necessary.

'What do we do? What the hell do we do?' Mike
exploded suddenly, his voice rising uncontrollably, just
as Judy was gripped by another contraction.

'You both do what these classes have just taught
you,' Juliet said very firmly. 'Work on your breathing
together. Stay on all fours, Judy. That will help to take
the pressure of the baby's weight off that cord. There
was no meconium staining in your waters and that's a
good sign that the baby wasn't in distress a few minutes
ago. But those contractions are starting to push the
head down into the birth canal where it might compress
the cord, so I'm going to try and counteract that by
holding the baby back. It's going to be uncomfortable
for both of us. . .'

'Dr Beckhill is on his way to the hospital,' Margaret
reported, 'and the ambulance should be here in less
than ten minutes. It's lucky I live so close to the
hospital.'

'Lucky that it happened here, then, instead of at our
place,' Mike said, more in control again now. 'We're
half an hour up into the hills.'

The minutes passed with terrible slowness, and
Judy's next contraction had accelerated in duration and
intensity. Margaret's brief manual examination told
them that the cord had not prolapsed any further, but
the two nurses were aware, even if the couple themselves were not, that damage might already have been
done. The lights and siren of the ambulance in the
driveway came as a blessed relief to all of them.

Margaret stayed behind while Juliet and Mike
accompanied Judy to the hospital in the speeding
vehicle, and then a battery of emergency staff took

over, trundling her down the corridors and up the lift as fast as possible to the obstetrics theatre, where surgical staff, anaesthetist and paediatrician were already scrubbed and waiting.

'There's a room just along here where fathers can wait,' Juliet said to Mike once Judy had been wheeled into the operating theatre.

Since there had been no time to lose, an epidural had been out of the question, and when a Caesarean was done under general anaesthesia fathers were not permitted to be present. Mike could have watched at a distance through the soundproof glass that separated the theatre from the fluorescent-lit corridor, but Juliet steered him away without mentioning this, guessing that he was too upset to witness the surgery from such a helpless position.

'Will it be long?'

'No, amazingly quick, actually. You'll barely have time to sit down,' she answered, then, seeing his pale face and the trembling he was trying vainly to control, she added, 'Would you like me to wait with you?'

'Do you. . .? If you——'

'I want to wait anyway,' she said firmly, 'to see that baby who's giving us all this trouble!'

He was clearly relieved to have a companion and paced up and down, talking jitterily. 'Margaret said in the class that about one in five women have a Caesarean these days, which made it almost certain that one of us ten couples would,' he said. 'And we were so determined it wouldn't be Judy. We were going into this with such a positive attitude. We really wanted the natural experience. And now. . .'

'Something happened which you couldn't possibly have predicted,' Juliet said. 'Don't question the Caesarean. It was vital.'

She didn't add that it still might not be enough, and a minute or two more passed very slowly, until she said, 'Here, grab the gown out of this pack and put it on. They'll probably want you to wear it when you hold your baby.'

Mike Minster donned the blue cotton garment and added the cap that the pack also contained, then they went back along the corridor and looked through the glass.

'What. . .? Is that. . .?' Mike gasped, and at the same time Juliet caught sight of the baby too—a wriggling red creature with its mouth wide open in a healthy yell, obviously only a minute or two old.

One of the nurses saw them at that moment and mouthed, 'It's a girl,' as she made an 'A-OK' sign with her thumb, and Mike leaned weakly against the glass, almost crying with relief.

'I was so afraid,' he said.

'Things did get a bit hair-raising there,' Juliet admitted. 'But now. . . Congratulations! As soon as the paediatrician has checked her over and the nurse has cleaned her up you'll be able to go next door to the nursery and hold her in your arms.'

'And Judy. . .?'

'It'll take quite a bit longer to close the incision that it did to open it, but when she's safely in Recovery, you and the baby can both go in too. She'll be very groggy, though.'

When he had gone to meet his new little daughter, and Juliet had made a quick call to Margaret to tell her the news, she was left feeling rather let down. She could see Hugh still absorbed in closing Judy's incision. They had not met face to face this evening, as he had already been scrubbed and in the theatre by the time she arrived at the labour ward. It would be easy and sensible simply to slip away, but instead she remained at the window for some moments longer, watching the silent pantomime of surgery.

Now that the baby was safe, the tension had lifted and the group of professionals gathered around Judy's sleeping form had time for some conversation and a joke or two, even as they concentrated carefully on everything they did. Hugh looked tired, she thought, and not entirely happy. The pretty dark-haired scrub nurse who stood next to him was trying to draw him out, but without a great deal of success, it seemed. He was probably simply anxious to go home.

Which was exactly what Juliet herself should do, as it was now after eleven, and she would have to find a taxi to take her to Margaret's, where she would collect her car. As she was thinking this, however, Hugh looked up and saw her for the first time.

'Wait,' he mouthed, and she nodded. He should only be a few more minutes.

It was in fact about five minutes later that he emerged, leaving other members of the team to move Judy from table to stretcher.

'Hi,' he said, on a tired sigh as he pulled off cap and mask. 'I heard something about Judy coming in the ambulance with her childbirth instructor and guessed it was you. If you and Margaret hadn't picked up the problem so quickly, it might have been tragic. Thanks.'

'It was Judy hersef who felt that something was wrong,' Juliet answered as they began to walk along the corridor together. 'Once we examined her and found out that her instinct was right, it was pretty clear what we had to do.'

'OK, in that case, I'm glad you took her fears seriously. Some people might have just put them down to first-time nerves.'

'Well, we knew her fairly well after four weeks of childbirth classes. She's the kind of person who does a lot of reading and was very well-informed about the whole process of pregnancy and birth.'

'Yes, some doctors prefer their patients *not* to be quite so well-informed, but I must say it usually seems to me to be to everyone's advantage if a woman knows what's going on.'

They paused, having reached the room where Hugh needed to change, and Juliet began awkwardly, 'Goodnight, then, Hugh. I'm glad I was able to——'

'Hang on,' he interrupted. 'You came in the ambulance. How are you getting home?'

'I'll take a taxi to Margaret's and pick up my car there.'

'No, you won't. Wait, and I'll give you a lift. . .and don't open your mouth like that, ready to utter a lot of polite protestations.'

'All right,' she conceded on a laugh. 'I'd like a lift. Thanks.'

And so it happened that she found herself in that low forest-green Jaguar once again, when she had spent the last weeks convincing herself that this kind of intimacy had gone between them forever. Not that a five-minute car ride was a particularly intimate thing, she reminded herself as they sat beside one another, enveloped in the throaty hum of the expensive engine.

Not particularly intimate, and it passed all too quickly. It seemed that Hugh had made just one very bland remark about the weather when the car was already cruising to a steady halt in front of Margaret's darkened house, the powerful beams of the Jaguar's headlights glowing against the red rear reflectors of Juliet's own very modest vehicle parked directly ahead.

He didn't switch off the engine, and sat there still

gripping the steering-wheel, staring straight ahead so that Juliet had to lean forward to look at him as she said her hesitant thanks and goodnight.

'It was no trouble,' was all he said in response, and she left the car, bitter with herself because those few bland, meaningless moments alone with him had been far too important to her.

'I must get over this,' she said to herself desperately as she took the wheel of her own vehicle. 'We went out together a couple of times and we see each other at work. I can't be in love with him. I *won't* be!'

But, as she looked in her rear-view mirror and watched the Jaguar pull smoothly away from the kerb and pass beyond her into the night, she knew that she was.

CHAPTER SEVEN

'IT WAS lovely to see you at the wine launch with Hugh,' said Alicia Beckhill as Juliet noted down her blood-pressure reading.

'Yes, it was a wonderful night,' Juliet answered, wilfully misunderstanding. 'You and David must be very pleased.'

'Oh, we were so nervous beforehand, and of course my father-in-law didn't help. But I really meant. . . well, your engagement to David was over a long time ago. I hated you quite a bit when David and I first started going out together, but now, if you and Hugh are getting serious about each other I couldn't be happier.'

'Oh. . .!' Juliet gasped through a sudden lump in her throat, then she mastered herself and continued in what she hoped was the right tone of ease and casualness. 'Please! Don't get it wrong, Alicia. Hugh and I are just colleagues and friends, nothing more.' Then she improvised, hoping very much that she wouldn't be caught out in the lie later on. 'He. . .his. . .the woman he originally asked to the wine launch had intestinal flu that night and couldn't go, so I stepped in. That's all it was.'

'Really? Oh. All right. I hope I didn't embarrass you, then.' Alicia looked genuinely disappointed, and Juliet suddenly decided to her own surprise that she could like David Beckhill's wife quite a bit if they were ever to get the chance to become friends—which they wouldn't, of course.

Although pampered since her wedding to the Beckhill heir, and probably long before that, she somehow had a simplicity of nature that put her beyond the social bitchery Juliet remembered so well from her own more glamorous days.

'No, you didn't embarrass me,' she said carefully. 'But tell me, how are you feeling? No problems, nothing unusual?'

'Well, I'm not very keen on this Clomid. Or maybe it's the Pergonal. Who knows? Perhaps it isn't the fertility drugs at all, but I've been feeling horribly tired for the past week or so, since we got back from overseas. I suppose it could be a low-grade virus I've picked up somewhere, couldn't it?'

'Perhaps,' Juliet answered cautiously, not wanting to offer a definite opinion. 'You'd better mention it to Hugh.'

'Oh, I will. And I'll probably burst into tears when I do. I've got hideous PMS today. Is he ready for me now?'

'Yes, I think I just heard Mrs Angstrom leaving. I'll check.' Juliet knocked on the light wooden door that connected the examining-room to Hugh Beckhill's office and popped her head inside on hearing his response. 'Are you ready for the next patient?' she said, deliberately using the impersonal phrase rather than Alicia's name. It was part of a constant vigilance she kept these days on her manner, her speech, anything that happened when she was with Hugh. So far, in the six weeks since the wine launch, this vigilance hadn't really helped.

'Yes, I'll be right in,' was his absent reply, and he didn't look up at her, seemingly immersed in the latest medical journal that had arrived that morning.

'All right.' Then, foolishly, she allowed herself to

linger for just one unnecessary second—enough time to notice all the things about him that disturbed her senses all day long. A lock of his thick, slightly silver-threaded brown hair fell across his forehead as he studied a closely printed article, one lean-fingered hand drummed a light tattoo on the polished surface of his desk, and she couldn't help remembering how that clean hair had felt in her hands and brushing against her face, and how expertly those hands had drawn a sensual response from her with their caresses.

Quickly, and with too loud a click, she closed the door again and turned to Alicia. 'Yes, he's on his way,' she said, then left the room and went to the testing-room where Alicia's latest pregnancy test should now be giving a result.

Alicia herself hadn't seemed concerned about the test this month, hadn't created any false pregnancy symptoms for herself, and had had signs that her period was about to start any minute. The test and the infertility treatment itself were becoming routine, and when Juliet saw the result on the HCG reaction disk it didn't even register for a few moments. She had her pen poised over Alicia's patient notes ready to write the word 'Positive' before it clicked. The test said that Alicia was pregnant!

Juliet's first impulse was to rush like a crazy woman to Hugh's office, fling open the door and call out the wonderful word, 'Positive!' for the whole building to hear, but then she stopped and thought more carefully. This wasn't the result of a blood-test, just a simple urine test of which she performed several every week. The results were not always accurate, and, although false negatives were more common than false positives, the latter could never be completely ruled out. Alicia

had not complained of any other pregnancy symptoms
. . .or had she?

She had spoken of a 'virus', or a negative reaction to
the mild fertility drugs she had been taking, and had
talked of premenstrual stress. Looked at from another
angle, those were classic pregnancy symptoms,
although they did not leap to people's minds the way
nausea and sensitivity to foods and odours did. Even
so, Juliet did not want to risk creating false hopes.

I'll have to talk to Hugh about it first, she realised,
and although it was tempting to put off the moment
when she had to be alone with him here she knew that
she should not.

'Hugh, I need to see you for a minute,' she said to
him seconds later. He nodded calmly before excusing
himself to Alicia and followed Juliet into the testing-
room.

Then, before she could speak, he said, 'You're going
to tell me that the test result was positive, aren't you?'

'Yes!'

He had pulled her towards him before she knew
what was happening, lifting her off her feet in an
exuberant hug that left her with breathless lungs and a
pounding heart. A moment later, she was back on the
ground and he was as cool as ever. 'Thank heavens for
that!' he said. 'At last!'

'Then you don't think it could be a false result? That
fatigue she mentioned, the idea of a virus, and the
PMS symptoms——'

'Are all good solid pregnancy symptoms,' he finished
for her, still visibly joyful about the news. 'She's even
a couple of days late with her period now, but she's
been so convinced it would come any moment, with
the bloated, headachy, moody feelings she's been

having, that she hasn't made the connection at all. I'll do a blood-test as well, but I'm pretty convinced.'

'Hugh, that's fabulous!' Juliet exclaimed sincerely, thinking only of the fact that an infertile couple had successfully conceived at last.

His sudden change of mood came as a shock. 'You're pleased?' he said distantly. 'I wasn't sure that you would be.'

'Of course I'm——'

Too late. He had already gone, and after that veiled accusation he had made she didn't have the heart to go and witness Alicia's response to the news she had hoped for for so long. Instead, she returned to the waiting-room and called Dr Steinbeck's next patient.

Alicia emerged from Hugh's office five minutes later in a glowing daze of disbelief and happiness. She would come in next week with David for a more detailed examination and discussion with Hugh about the pregnancy. Catching sight of Juliet in the testing-room as the latter searched in the cupboard for a sample tube of anti-candida ointment that Dr Gordon had asked for, she paused in the doorway, brimming with tears.

'Oh, Juliet!' she said. 'I can't believe it! It's the first month in three and a half years that I haven't been counting the *minutes* that my period was late, and reading and re-reading the lists of pregnancy symptoms in half a dozen different books. David's been away quite a bit, promoting the new wine, and I've had to go with him on a couple of trips. We just got back from America ten days ago, and I thought perhaps that's why I was run down and out-of-kilter. David's in Sydney till tomorrow. I don't know whether to try and reach him at his hotel, or wait until he gets home.'

'Wait,' answered Juliet. 'Don't you want to see his face and feel his arms around you when you tell him?'

'Yes, you're right, I do,' Alicia nodded with a soft smile. 'But I don't know how I'll live through the hours till he's due back.'

'Start looking at baby name books,' Juliet advised lightly.

Alicia laughed. 'I will! That's *exactly* what I'll do!'

'I noticed one in a bookshop the other day,' Juliet said. 'It claimed to have something like twelve thousand names in it. That should keep you busy.'

The whole practice was infected by Alicia's happiness for the rest of the day. It was wonderful news when any infertility patient succeeded in conceiving, but Alicia's personal connection with Hugh made it all the better. Juliet's feelings were more complex, however. David would be over the moon, she knew, and she couldn't help wondering how things would have been if this had happened six months ago, before she had ever joined the practice and thus readmitted the Beckhill cousins into her life.

With his wife already happily pregnant, and no cloud hanging over his own fertility and completeness as a man, perhaps David would never have felt even a moment of rekindled interest in the fiancée he had last seen nearly nine years ago. And if David had not suggested that there were past issues still unresolved between them, perhaps Juliet's own feelings would have remained cold ashes, so that Hugh's doubts would have had nothing to cling to.

And Alicia might have been right, Juliet thought. Hugh and I might have become seriously involved.

But it was stupid and pointless to speculate over such distant might-have-beens. She had not come to the Barossa Valley in search of love, but in search of a more peaceful existence, and this she was certainly finding. She had joined a hiking group and was taking a quilt-making course one evening a week, and now that the warm weather was here friends from Adelaide would be coming up for weekend picnics and barbecues at nearby beauty spots or in the flower-filled garden of her own bluestone cottage.

And work here at the practice in Romneyvale was very pleasant. Judy Minster had recovered well from the birth of eight-pound Theodora, and three more women from her childbirth group had now had their babies, all with no major intervention and all largely drug free.

'Do you have any particular plans for Alicia's pre-natal care?' Juliet asked Hugh later that afternoon after she had brought him the pathology lab results that had just arrived.

'There's no reason why it shouldn't be an easy and completely normal pregnancy and delivery,' Hugh replied, looking up from the print-out she had just handed him. Then he added, 'Having said that, I *am* going to advise extra rest and care with diet and exercise. She can afford to take things easy, and make the effort to have a healthy lifestyle—and after waiting this long for a baby, she'll want to do everything to ensure a trouble-free pregnancy.'

Juliet nodded and took in a nervous breath. What she wanted to say now was not going to be easy. 'Hugh, I was angry about what you said earlier.'

'What was that?' He focused on her more closely, narrowing his eyes.

'Your suggestion that I wasn't pleased about Alicia's news,' she replied steadily, meeting his gaze. 'I'd have to be pretty low to feel that way, no matter what personal stake I had in the matter—and in fact I have no personal stake at all. I was hurt, actually, as well as angry, that you could think that of me.'

There was a silence, then he said in a low tone, 'Hurt, Juliet?'

'Yes. I thought that, even though what. . .started to happen between us two months ago was a mistake. . .' she chose the word with care and pronounced it firmly '. . .at least it had ended with no hard feelings. I don't feel badly towards you. At least, I didn't. Now, I'm not so sure.'

He rose from behind the large desk and at first she thought he was going to come towards her, but instead he turned away and went to the window, fingering the crimson damask curtains absently as he stared out into the lush shrubbery beyond the glass.

Finally, he wheeled around and spoke. 'Yes. You're right. It was a petty comment on my part, and untrue as well, I'm sure.'

'Then what made you say it?' she pressed, and suddenly he was upon her, two hard hands gripping her shoulders.

'Damn it, Juliet!' His face was only inches from hers, and his hazel eyes, normally warm and open, burned with an emotion she could not read. 'Must we pick apart our feelings like this? I said it. I was wrong. I'm sorry. That's enough, isn't it?'

She was still too shocked by his sudden attack to find a reply, and before she could even begin to struggle for words his hands had slid from her shoulders to her back, his arms closing around her like moulded steel bars. His mouth pressed against her hair and then he searched for her face, coaxing her lips to meet his own in a hot, heedless kiss that left her breathless within seconds.

She didn't want to respond to him—her head didn't, that was. Her body and her heart simply couldn't help it, and his kiss tasted like water must taste after dry hours in the desert. She crumbled inside with a longing to taste more of him and to know the texture of his skin against her most sensitive flesh. Only the knowledge that there were patients waiting and a whole surgery building full of medical activity just outside that closed oak door gave her the strength to pull away from him, and he released her at the same time so that suddenly they were feet apart again, both breathing heavily. His eyes, meeting hers, seemed distant and hostile.

'You'd better go,' he said, chilly and wooden, and she nodded silently, appalled at how a kiss, which was supposed to bring people closer together, had only, it seemed, driven them further apart.

'David! What are you doing here?' Juliet exclaimed in surprise, early the next afternoon, coming towards him across the waiting-room as he stood uncertainly by the front desk.

No one was waiting at the moment—a miraculous respite that only occurred about once a fortnight—and Debbie was on the phone, while Jeannette, the agency nurse replacing Margaret while the latter took her holiday, was weighing a patient ready for Dr Gordon. Congratulations on Alicia's new pregnancy leaped to Juliet's smiling lips, but an impulse told her to stifle them for a moment longer—wisely, as it turned out.

'I've come straight from the airport,' he answered. 'Just back from Sydney.'

'So you haven't seen Alicia yet?'

'No. Why?'

'I just wondered. . .why you wanted to come straight here, that's all,' she explained lamely. 'Nothing wrong, I hope.'

'The opposite, actually,' David said. 'In Sydney

someone was telling me about a new fertility treatment that sounds perfect for Alicia and I wanted to talk to Hugh about it straight away. Didn't want to mention it to Alicia first in case it didn't apply to her problem and I got her hopes up for nothing.'

As usual, he was dismissing his own part in the problem, although Alicia had said yesterday that he had been carefully following the simple steps towards raising his sperm count that Hugh had outlined to him several weeks earlier—a healthy diet, regular exercise, as little alcohol as someone in his business could get away with, and dressing in loose cotton underwear and trousers. It was very possible, although he didn't know it yet, that these small things were what had tipped the balance and allowed Alicia to conceive.

'Right. Of course,' Juliet answered him helplessly after a pause, which she hoped he hadn't noticed. It wasn't her place, nor Hugh's, to give away Alicia's marvellous news, and she didn't envy Hugh having to navigate his way tactfully through the coming interview. In fact, if she could put David off somehow. . .

'Why don't I mention it to him and you can come back later when he's free?' she suggested. 'Then he'll have had a chance to——'

She broke off as Hugh himself strolled into the waiting-room behind his departing patient. 'Nobody waiting? Hello, David. Congr——'

'David's come straight from the airport,' Juliet interjected quickly, telegraphing a warning with her blue eyes.

Hugh bit back the word and looked as uncomfortable as Juliet had felt moments before.

'Yes, I wanted to see you straight away,' David came in, taking his cousin by the arm and propelling him through into the privacy of his office. He was too eager about what he wanted to discuss to have noticed Hugh's near slip. 'Have you heard of a new treatment called——?'

The heavy panelled door shut behind them, cutting off his words, and Juliet turned to greet one of Dr Steinbeck's patients, who had just entered. Cecily Travers, a patient of Dr Gordon's who was about to become a mother for the first time at the age of forty-two, followed close behind, signalling that the unaccustomed lull was well and truly broken.

David left Hugh's office just as Juliet was weighing Mrs Travers—although 'left' was not really the right word. 'Catapulted' might have been a more accurate description. He left the door swinging open and half turned to shout back at Hugh, heedless of witnesses, 'We'll go to someone else, Hugh, if necessary. I mean that.'

If the obstetrician gave a reply, Juliet didn't hear it above the slamming of the door. David turned on his heel and came face to face with her as she stood with Cecily Travers at the heavy medical scales. Unwisely, she attempted to soothe him down, but he barked at her before she was halfway through the first phrase, 'Is it any of your business? Think about it. Is it?'

'N-no, David, it isn't. I'm sorry.'

He strode on through the door to the waiting-room and out of the building.

'Excuse me a moment, Mrs Travers,' Juliet murmured to the older woman, who was a little shaken by witnessing David's anger.

She slipped into Hugh's office to find him standing somewhat helplessly behind his desk.

"I didn't handle that at all well,' he said woodenly, and Juliet had to smile.

'I didn't either. I tried to calm him down as he left,

and he said, quite rightly, that it wasn't my business. I gather, then, that the treatment he'd heard about isn't something you would recommend.'

'No!'

'But couldn't you have played along? As soon as he gets home he'll find Alicia bursting with her news.'

'Perhaps I *should* have played along,' he acknowledged, meeting her eyes at last. 'I would have done if it had been a well-researched and widely recognised treatment, but unfortunately it's not. Vern, Geoffrey and myself have all read about it and all come to the conclusion that it's hocus-pocus. David only heard about it through someone—not a medical professional, and with only third-hand experience—singing its praises at a dinner party. I found I couldn't pretend enthusiasm about the idea even for a few minutes. Those sort of white lies can backfire in unexpected ways, I've found.'

'Well, at least this particular bomb should be defused pretty soon,' Juliet concluded, and he nodded rueful agreement as she turned to go, absurdly pleased, after yesterday's brief, burning kiss, because it hadn't been a hostile exchange.

'Juliet? It's Alicia Beckhill here.'

The phone had rung just moments after Juliet entered her house, and she had barely had time to change her clothes, let alone fed Spats, who was weaving impatient figure-eights around her bare, smooth legs.

'Hello, Alicia,' Juliet answered, trying not to betray surprise at the call. 'How are you?' She felt a moment's foreboding. Could the longed-for pregnancy be in trouble this early?

But Alicia's voice was calm and happy. 'I'm fine, as

I hope you'll be able to see for yourself in half an hour or so. David and I would love it if you'd come round for a drink—David because he wants to apologise for exploding at you today, me because I'm so happy that I want to see people and celebrate. . .with non-alcoholic champagne, needless to say.'

'I'd love to come. Alicia, Thank you,' Juliet answered, not sure if it was the truth, but wanting to respond to the other woman's infectious happiness. 'As long as you're not putting yourself out for me. And I'll accept David's apology without champagne as a bribe. Will anyone else be there?'

'Just Hugh, and no, we're *not* putting ourselves out, I promise. David wants to apologise to him, too.'

Just Hugh. . . Damn! Why hadn't she found a way of eliciting this information before she committed herself? Juliet thought. But it was too late now.

'Half an hour, did you say?' she asked thinly.

'Whenever,' Alicia answered. 'If you need longer, don't rush. . .'

'Half an hour is fine,' Juliet assured her, thinking that the sooner the drinks hour was over the better.

After scooping Spat's food somewhat carelessly into his bowl and pouring him fresh water, she hurried to her room to riffle through her wardrobe, knowing that she couldn't turn up in the old Nile-green blouse and skirt she was wearing now. After some indecision, she finally chose suede trousers in a soft French grey and a hand-knitted white top in a patchwork of luxurious yarns—silk, angora, linen and Lurex.

Low-heeled grey shoes and a simple strand of pearls, as well as freshened make-up and hair brushed into a glossy auburn halo, completed the outfit, and she hoped she had struck the right balance between the casualness suggested by the impromptu invitation and the formality that seemed to automatically attach itself to anything connected with the Beckhill estate.

Hugh had not yet arrived when she was ushered into the small suite that Alicia and David used for private entertaining, and she started to hope that he would be called out. A threesome of David, Alicia and herself might be awkward, but not as awkward as a foursome that included David's cousin.

In theory, Lloyd and Barbara Beckhill lived in this enormous house, too, but in fact they spent far more time these days at their large town house in North Adelaide. When they were home, they mainly used their own rooms on the second floor, so Juliet had little expectation of their expanding the gathering.

'Juliet!' David came forward as she entered, and grasped her hands eagerly. 'Do you forgive today?'

'Of course I do.'

'I've been going round like a bear with a sore head over this thing for months now. I know that, and I'm ashamed of it, but. . .can you see how the problem we've had strikes right at the roots of everything that's important? It starts to overshadow the simple desire for a baby and becomes something even deeper.'

'Yes, I do see,' Juliet answered sincerely.

'And being aware that too many people know, and that they're talking about it, feeling their pity, or their ridicule, feeling angry at anyone who conceives easily, or, worse, the people who conceive when they didn't even want a child.'

'I know. I see it with other couples we work with at the practice, and some of them are far more difficult than you've been, in all sorts of different ways. Anger, depression, denial, resentment.'

'Casting about for the most ridiculous false solutions,' he put in, and she suspected he was thinking about the times he had tried to rekindle their own relationship. Wisely, she didn't acknowledge this.

'Please don't blame yourself for any of those feelings,' she said instead.

'Can I get you a drink, then, now that the humble pie is out of the way?'

'Yes, please.'

'Alicia's given the go-ahead on champagne, although she won't share it. Would that be all right?'

'I'd love to have a toast to the baby, yes.'

'Good, and here's Hugh.'

'Did I hear the word "champagne"?'

To Juliet, his presence seemed to dominate the pale, exquisitely decorated room, pushing her hosts into the background. They greeted each other with careful friendliness and made a couple of obvious remarks about whether he might be called out, then David started talking to Hugh about some winery business and Alicia turned to Juliet, full of plans about the baby, and things became easier.

'Come to my office for a minute and I'll show you,' David said to Hugh after several minutes. Their discussion was very technical, involving plans for new equipment in the winery itself, and Juliet had not made head nor tail of the snatches of sentences that had come to her ears.

The two men left, and she was now alone with Alicia. The latter only waited till the door had closed behind them before saying, in an abrupt change of subject, 'I like your outfit.'

'Thank you.'

Alicia had been sitting back comfortably agianst the white wool couch, still obviously feeling the fatigue of early pregnancy in spite of her happiness about it, but now she sat forward, making Juliet shift herself so that she was perched more precariously on the matching armchair.

'Now, Juliet,' the other woman said firmly, 'I want to know what's going on with you and Hugh—and no more white lies about another woman who wasn't available at the last moment. I asked Hugh about her and he didn't know what I was talking about.'

'Nothing's going on,' Juliet said, hot and uncomfortable. She thought about what Hugh himself had said only that day—that white lies had a way of backfiring unexpectedly. He was right, and her denial wasn't good enough for Alicia.

'Excuse me,' she said, 'but something *is*. That, or else one of you wants there to be.'

'What makes you think that?' Juliet prevaricated desperately.

'Well, for one thing, the room was electric as soon as he walked in.'

'Was it? I——'

'I know I'm pestering horribly, but I'd love it if Hugh found someone. He's had bad luck with women over the past few years. One was only interested in the Beckhill connection, another one told him her last boyfriend was out of the picture and then all of a sudden upped and married him, and the third was very sweet but just all wrong for him. He had a crush on you nine years ago. . .'

'Oh, no, that couldn't be right. . .' Ironic if her spoilt assumption back then that he had loved her from afar turned out now to be correct, when it was far too late to do anything about it.

'But he did, Juliet. Then he forgot about you for years until you suddenly turned up. It seems too good to be true, and since I'm such a romantic. . .especially now. . .please tell me that there's a future in it. . .?'

She cocked her blonde head winningly to one side and Juliet shook her own slowly. 'I'm sorry, Alicia. It's not going to be like that. You're right, we were. . . starting to go out together around the time of the wine launch, but we found that it wasn't working. Quite an amicable decision, fortunately, but definitely not a romantic one.'

Alicia studied her closely for several uncomfortable seconds then muttered, 'What on earth is Hugh doing? He's a fool. . .'

And while Juliet was still feeling completely naked in the light of the other woman's ability to read her feelings so clearly, the men returned, their relaxation with one another flowing warmly through the room in contrast to the moments of tension Juliet had witnessed between them during Alicia's long struggle to conceive.

'Need a top-up on that champagne?' David asked.

'No, thanks, David,' Juliet said. 'I should get home.' Then, improvising quickly, 'I'm expecting my mother to ring from Perth tonight.' Another of those white lies! Her mother probably *would* ring, but Juliet didn't usually sit at home waiting for the call.

'Hugh?'

'No, not for me. I'm on call and there are things I need to get done at home.'

'I was hoping I'd persuade you both to stay to dinner,' Alicia said, disappointed.

Juliet, feeling herself stiffen at the way the other woman had coupled her with Hugh, saw that he, too, had reacted against Alicia's choice of words.

'Well, I can't speak for Juliet,' he said, 'but I really do have to go myself.'

He rose, as if wanting to make a quick getaway alone, but Alicia and David immediately began shepherding both him and Juliet towards the door. They were only being polite hosts, escorting their guests out, but it had the effect, once again, of forcing the two medical colleagues together, and Juliet saw at once that Hugh was as uncomforatble about it as she was.

There was no choice, however, but to go politely along, making more conversation as they proceeded rather slowly down the spotless Nile green carpet of the passage and into the main entrance hall where the dark wood of the polished floor glowed waxily.

'I'm glad you could both come,' Alicia said when they reached the big double doors at last. She patted her still very flat stomach with a soft smile. 'I'd like to have a party for five hundred to celebrate this, but I know that's foolish.'

'Yes, Alicia,' Hugh said seriously. 'Take it easy over the next few months until the danger of early miscarriage is past.'

'You don't have to tell me!' She took his arm and gave him a squeeze, then pulled him gently in Juliet's direction and propelled them both down the marble steps so that there was little they could do but walk side by side to their cars.

'She's very happy,' Juliet said unnecessarily, simply to break the silence.

'Yes,' Hugh answered absently.

It was a beautiful evening, just approaching sunset, and the landscaped flowerbeds, shrubberies, rose garden and treed lawns glowed with vivid greens and warm pinks, mauves and yellows in the late, slanting light. Juliet had never really explored the Beckhill estate gardens before, and she knew a sudden impulse to say to Hugh, 'Let's go for a walk.' She remembered how relaxed they had been together that afternoon two months ago in the hills—she hadn't yet lit the candles he had given her that day—and wondered helplessly why that mood between them had so thoroughly gone. It would be impossible to suggest a walk together.

He had already got out his keys, although they had not yet reached the gravelled parking space, and was jangling them loudly in his hand as if impatient to be away. A slant of sun caught at his hair as they stood beside their respective car doors, bringing out golden lights in the dark brown, making his skin glow and crisping the whiteness of his shirt collar against his tanned neck.

'See you tomorrow,' he said woodenly.

Then, as they climbed into their cars, Juliet heard Alicia's voice behind her, calling clearly from the steps. 'Goodnight!'

She and David had stayed to wave them off, and if Alicia had still been cherishing any romantic hopes for her husband's ex-fiancée and cousin the stiff walk and minimal goodnight they had exchanged would surely put her off and save Juliet from any further painful match-making plans.

Now if only I can forget about it myself, Juliet thought wearily as she followed Hugh's Jaguar down the white gravelled driveway.

CHAPTER EIGHT

'Brr! There's definitely an autumn chill in the air today,' Margaret Chatham said as she entered the waiting-room one Friday morning in early April. 'Summer has gone on so late this year that I didn't even check the temperature, just left the house in my short sleeves, and now I'm freezing.'

'You're not sorry that summer has ended, though, are you?' Juliet asked. She had arrived several minutes ago and had put the kettle on for the cup of tea that both Dr Gordon and Dr Steinbeck liked as soon as they came in.

'Sorry? No! It's a relief—or it would be if I'd worn a cardigan or a jacket. Summer was stinking this year, the hottest and longest for a long time, I'd say.'

'One thing I have missed about Adelaide,' Juliet said, 'is being able to go down to the suburban beaches for a picnic tea and a sunset swim. The Romneyvale municipal pool can't quite compete.'

'But you are enjoying the job and the lifestyle here, aren't you?' Margaret Chatham said with a sharp glance. 'You've been here about eight months now, and sometimes I've wondered if you felt the move had been a mistake.'

'No, not at all,' Juliet answered quickly. 'I enjoy it here very much—both the job and the Barossa Valley itself.'

'The romance that was beginning to bloom for you several months ago—forgive me if I'm prying, but perhaps that didn't turn out quite as you were hoping?'

141

'It was a disappointment, yes,' Juliet said evenly. 'But it's over now, and I'm back on an even keel.'

'I thought there was something,' the older woman said, touching Juliet's arm sympathetically. 'There were times over the summer when I thought it was more than the heat that was getting you down. It's hard, isn't it? And you can't always avoid meeting the person afterwards.'

'Yes, it *is* hard.' Did Margaret suspect that it was Hugh?

'I didn't want to say anyting, but——'

'It's fine,' Juliet assured her. 'You're not prying. It's nice to know that a friend is concerned, and it really is over, with no lasting harm done.'

There were moments, in fact, when this was still not quite the truth, but by and large Juliet was very happy now. Recently she had been out to dinner and a film with a very nice geologist, Chris Taylor, whom she had met through the local hiking club, and he had invited her out again this weekend to an evening of fondue and wine tasting. She was looking forward to it, and if it couldn't quite make up for the fact that an unknown female voice had phoned three times lately to ask with a throaty and slightly accented purr, 'Is Hugh there, please?', it definitely helped.

Alicia Beckhill was now a healthy six and a half months into her pregnancy, and looking more relaxed at every appointment now that morning sickness and the fear of early miscarriage had passed. If the baby was born now, it would have a good chance of survival, but there was no reason to fear that it would be born prematurely, as everything was going so well.

In the months since the celebration drink at the Beckhill estate, Juliet had not seen David at all. He had been in to the surgery twice, once to hear the baby's heartbeat and once to be present at the ultra-sound scan that had been done at sixteen weeks, but both times Juliet had been out on an errand, and she found that she didn't mind missing him. Alicia always chatted in a friendly way, and it seemed that the stresses in their marriage, caused by their long wait for a child, had now healed over. It was becoming increasingly easy to forget that there had ever been a connection between herself and Alicia's husband.

Later that chilly day, Chris Taylor called the surgery to confirm Saturday night's outing. 'Should be just the evening for it, if this weather keeps up,' he said cheerfully.

'Yes, and I think it's going to,' Juliet answered. 'I heard a forecast this morning that predicted rain for the next week.'

'Well, we need it,' he answered. 'But it does put a damper on my other plan, which was that we go on an all-day hike on Sunday as well.'

'Oh—er—yes,' she said a little uncertainly. 'That *is* a pity.' She was free on Sunday, certainly, but wasn't sure that she wanted to spend a whole long day with Chris just yet, and was a bit taken aback that he seemed to be presuming her availability for the plan. And what was he saying now?

'If you like, we could make it a really early start and go somewhere in the lower Flinders Ranges. It probably won't be raining that far north. We could climb Mount Remarkable, and——'

'Chris, let's leave it for this weekend,' she put in desperately. 'We'll find a time when we can rely on the weather. . . And I'd better not talk any longer, actually, as there are several patients waiting.'

'Fine, I understand,' he said staunchly. 'I'll pick you up on Saturday at seven.'

'Yes. Lovely,' she answered, making an effort to be warmer, then added, 'Oh, and Chris, by the way, how should I dr——?'

Too late. He had hung up before hearing the tacked-on question about what she should wear, and she didn't feel comfortable enough with him—yet, at least—to ring him back about it. In any case, there were those waiting patients, and Dr Gordon had just come in to the waiting-room rather impatiently to collect the next one on his list himself. Her weight, blood-pressure and urinalysis would have to be done after Dr Gordon had seen her, which was definitely not the most efficient way of going about things.

By the end of the day, Debbie, Margaret and Juliet didn't need to tell each other that the senior obstetrician was in rather a bad mood. Eight months ago, Juliet had felt confident that she would work well with the somewhat fatherly man, and mostly she did, but these days of irritability and shortness of fuse seemed to be coming increasingly often lately, and she wasn't surprised when Margaret said to her quietly as they stood together in the testing-room, 'I must ask him if he's had a check-up lately. Doctors so often neglect their own health and ignore symptoms they'd recognise in anyone else. He'll probably bite my head off for suggesting it. . .'

'He certainly will if you mention it today!'

'Credit me with some tact, Juliet! I'll wait till the right moment. . .but I do wonder if he's feeling quite well.'

They each exchanged a guilty, wary glance two minutes later when Dr Gordon himself appeared in the doorway of the testing-room, his brow heavily creased and his glasses almost foggy with irritation. 'Mrs Porter still isn't here?'

'No, I'm afraid not,' Margaret said.

'Well, I'm going home.'

'Dr Steinbeck has a backlog, since he only got back from the hospital an hour ago, and he was wondering if you'd see Mrs——'

'Get Hugh to see her,' he cut in impatiently. 'I want to get home.'

'Very well, Dr Gordon.' Margaret didn't mention that Hugh was also behind this afternoon.

'If there's one thing I can't tolerate, it's patients who don't turn up and don't let us know.'

'Yes, she's fifteen minutes late, but——'

Too late for any further soothing phrases. Dr Gordon had left the doorway. There was a series of sounds as he collected his bag and coat, then the main front door, never used by patients, was opened with an impatient rattle and closed again with a distinct bang, and he was gone.

Three minutes after his stately white car pulled out into the street, Louise Porter arrived. 'I might have known it,' muttered Margaret to Juliet as they crossed paths between the waiting-room and Dr Steinbeck's office. 'Geoffrey is really too rushed. See if Hugh will fit her in.'

'If Sally Adams takes much longer, Hugh will be more behind than Geoffrey,' Juliet countered helplessly.

'And I can't stay back tonight,' Margaret said. 'My daughter has six schoolfriends coming for spaghetti and video movies, and I haven't even been to the shops yet.'

So it happened that when Hugh's last patient left at ten to six Juliet was the one who had stayed behind. She was tidying a few last things ready for the cleaner who came in on Saturday mornings when Hugh emerged from his office, his last bundle of patient files in hand. Seeing her, he said easily, 'Go home! I'll lock up.'

Then they both heard a car pulling into the rear car park and exchanged puzzled glances. 'Someone forgot something?' he suggested.

'I doubt it,' Juliet shook her head. 'I've checked everything now, and unless Geoffrey left his medical bag in his desk drawer. . .'

Footsteps sounded on the gravel and then on the slate entranceway and there were voices, too, one male and one female, and the latter was making alternate groans and pantings that sounded very familiar to the two medical professionals.

'Who on earth——?' Hugh began.

The door opened and Roger Bantry and his wife Lucy stood there, the latter gripping her husband and crying out as another pain took hold of her.

'We had car trouble,' Roger gasped. 'You wouldn't believe it, would you? The thing would only go ten miles an hour. Don't know if it's the rain. . . Don't know what's wrong with it. Where's Dr Gordon?'

'Dr Gordon?' Juliet said. 'He left well over an hour ago.'

'But. . .' Roger turned to his wife, his face screwed into a grimace of confusion. 'Darling, when you phoned him——?'

'But *you* phoned him!' Lucy Bantry said, more calm now that the contraction had eased. 'When I was in the shower. Didn't you?'

'No, I thought you did while I was taking your hospital bag to the car.' Roger turned to Hugh. 'Then no one knew we were on our way!'

'No. Oh, lord!' Hugh exclaimed, suppressing a sigh.

'Let's examine you quickly and see what's going on. Juliet. . .?'

With a nod she went to his examining-room and spread out a fresh sheet on the padded bench. Behind her, she heard Lucy Bantry groan again and start to breathe with focused energy, threatening to lose control. Roger was explaining, 'Dr Gordon told us he'd examine her at the office first no matter what, or what time she went into labour, because so often people get to the hospital too early, so we've been prepared all along to come here, and as you heard we both somehow assumed that the other one had phoned. I'd only just got home from work. We were busy ringing Elinor's baby-sitter, where she was this afternoon, and Lucy's mother to ask her to pick Elinor up. The thing is, her contractions are awfully close, aren't they? And——'

'I'm starting to want to push. I need to start pushing,' Lucy managed to say. Her panting had increased in urgency, and Juliet began to gather more equipment. It didn't seem very likely, the way things were going, that Mr and Mrs Bantry were going to get to the hospital just yet.

'Keep panting,' Hugh said quickly. 'Roger, help her. You learnt the technique in the classes.'

'We didn't do the classes this time. When Elinor was born——'

'Like this, Lucy,' Hugh came in. 'Like blowing out candles on a cake one by one. Very shallow.' He demonstrated quickly.

'That's right, I remember it now,' Roger said, and began to take the lead for his wife to follow as she resisted the urge to start pushing the baby out.

When the long contraction left her, the two men helped her to the bench and Roger stood behind her,

holding her back and shoulders against his chest while
Juliet searched frantically for pillows to make the
labouring woman more comfortable. Washing his
hands and then slipping them into gloves, Hugh managed to complete the manual examination seconds
before the next contraction took hold.

'Fully effaced, fully dilated,' he said. 'Head at plus
two station. Look, Roger, you can see the baby's hair.
Lucy, you're going to deliver right here.'

But Lucy was already straining to get the baby out,
her face darkening with the effort as the baby's head
crowned fully. Juliet, still gathering equipment, saw
the head slip back a little as the contraction ended, but
she knew that only a few more minutes of hard work
by Mrs Bantry would be enough.

And in fact on the next contraction, with some
strenuous pushes that brought roars from deep within
her diaphragm, Lucy pushed the head out and Hugh
held it gently as he delivered the shoulders and then
slid out the rest of the slippery, blue-tinged creature.

'A boy, everyone,' he said. 'He's beautiful.'

Since there had been no drugs given to the mother,
the baby was alert and took his first breath spon-
taneously, so that a miraculous glow of pink began to
travel outwards from torso to extremities, replacing the
first purplish tone. Dr Beckhill gently checked his
mouth and nose to make sure that the airway was fully
clear, and Juliet stepped in to make the five obser-
vations that made up the baby's Apgar score.

'Eight,' she announced, pleased. After five minutes,
the score would probably be up to ten, its maximum
value. With a cloth that she had warmed over the
electric radiator, Juliet gently wiped away some of the
vernix and birth fluid that still coated the newborn.

The baby's black hair stuck wetly to his moulded

head, and his mouth was open in a protest that quietened as he was gently laid on his mother's warm belly.

'Hello, Max,' she said softly, and brought him carefully to her breast, where he immediately opened his mouth and found what he was looking for, his sucking reflex already strong and well-developed. The stimulation of the sucking helped to contract Lucy's uterus so that the placenta slipped out easily and Hugh examined it and found that it was complete and healthy.

'I turned the heating on again, but the office is still not all that warm,' Juliet said. 'We don't have any baby blankets here, but we should put him in a towel or two.'

'Yes.' Hugh turned to her. 'Call an ambulance. Let's get these two comfortably installed in hospital. They can wash the baby more thoroughly there. Roger, you'll be able to go with them in the ambulance, so why don't you get your wife's hospital bag from the car? When you're ready, of course.'

Juliet slipped out to the phone and rang for an ambulance, which should arrive in about fifteen minutes' time. Then she returned to find the couple absorbed in their baby. Hugh said quietly to her, 'She didn't even tear, so there's nothing to do. I must call Vern. He'll want to come in and see her at the hospital, I imagine.'

Twenty minutes later, and just an hour after Mr and Mrs Bantry's surprising arrival, it was all over, leaving nothing but a few extra sheets and towels to consign to the laundry, and a few unexpected instruments to be sterilised. Having cast an eye over the place to make sure it was thoroughly tidy and switched off the heating again, Juliet picked up her bag and black wool jacket ready to leave.

Hugh was standing in the entranceway. 'All locked up and switched off?' he said.

'I hope so. I checked extra-thoroughly. After an event like this, it's easy to forget something.'

'After an event like this, I'm feeling hungry,' he answered. 'Would you like to have dinner? There's a new Italian place opened up in Hazelton that's supposed to be good.'

'Oh, I——'

'If there's no good reason to say no, then say yes, because we both need it,' he put in, before she had considered her answer. His light touch on her arm immediately began to undo months of careful work on her feelings.

'Italian sounds lovely,' she said lightly, betraying none of her doubts. 'I'm starving.'

'Let's both take our cars,' he suggested. 'It'd be out of the way to come back here afterwards to collect one of them.'

The practical suggestion reassured her a little. This was two people who worked together taking a quick bite after a long day. Nothing more, and she had nothing to fear—or hope—from him. 'Shall I follow you, or will you give me directions?' she asked

'How about both, just in case we get split up by a convoy of trucks? It's called the Olive Grove and it's in Torrens Street, opposite the Southern Cross Hotel.'

'The Southern Cross. . . That big old place with the iron lace all round its veranda?'

'That's the one.'

But in fact she did manage to follow him all the way and they parked next to one another in the reserved area beside the restaurant building. Like many places in the Barossa Valley, it was an old building made of distinctive South Australian stone, this time not bluestone like her own cottage, but an earthy ochre, trimmed with rust-red brick.

Inside, there was mellow light and subdued country-style décor, and Juliet was a little perturbed when the waiter cast an expert eye over them and ushered them to the most secluded of the tables for two, in a corner near the stone fireplace which was alight with leaping flames, since the night was even chillier than the chilly day had been. This meal had the dangerous potential to be far too pleasant!

They ordered an antipasto to share, followed by a small serving of fettuccini with pesto sauce, then both decided on veal, with a lemon sauce for Hugh and a mushroom and wine sauce for Juliet. The waiter mentioned a couple of wines to them and had just returned a few minutes later to take their order for drinks when he was bustled aside by an older man with a small, pointed beard and a slightly over-developed middle.

'Go and see to table four,' he said peremptorily to the junior waiter, then changed his manner abruptly to a syrupy lilt as he greeted Hugh. 'Dr Beckhill! This is a real pleasure. You're still looking at the wine list, I see. We have a very good selection from your family firm. . .'

'Actually, I thought we'd try this Chablis,' Hugh said, holding the wine album open and pointing to the pastel-toned label of a very small new winery whose neat, sloping vineyards bordered Juliet's own cottage on one side.

'Oh! Of course!' The restaurant owner, as Juliet assumed he must be, looked a little taken aback but quickly recovered his over-smooth *savoir-faire*. 'Assessing the competition tonight, are you? You've chosen a good wine, naturally. An *excellent* wine.'

'Yes. I hope so. We'll see,' Hugh answered shortly,

and to his further annoyance the man backed deferentially away with an exaggerated performance of respecting Hugh's evident desire to be left alone.

'I hate that sort of thing!' he said in a low growl as soon as the owner had gone.

'I know.'

'I met him a few months ago, and if I'd realised this was the place he owned we would have gone somewhere else. I'm sorry.'

'It's worse for you than me,' Juliet assured him. 'Since it obviously happens to you regularly.'

'Was I very ungracious?'

'Only to the same extent that he was horribly obsequious.'

'Perhaps it wouldn't annoy me if I was in "the family firm", as he put it, but I'm not. I'm an obstetrician, and he knew that, yet he still treated me like an emissary of Uncle Lloyd.'

'Perhaps because that's how your uncle Lloyd treats you as well.'

He looked at her sharply. 'Perceptive, aren't you? I think you're right.'

She was absurdly pleased and said quickly, to hide the evidence of her pleasure in the form of pinkened cheeks, 'Don't let it stop you from relaxing.'

He focused his gaze on her once again. 'You mean, "Stop grumbling and say something interesting"?'

'No, I *didn't* meant that!' she laughed, and the tension was broken for a moment, but he quickly resumed the thoughtful, searching expression that moulded his face into smooth yet sombre planes.

She watched him and realised that this mood was not something he was going to shake off easily. Perhaps he needed a listener. . .

'What's on your mind, Hugh?' she asked softly. 'It's

not really the fact that people fawn over the Beckhill name, is it?'

'No,' he said, studying the flickering yellow flame of the low candle that burned between them, so that his dark lashes formed crescents against his tanned skin. 'That little incident just seemed to cap a different problem, I suppose. What did you think about tonight's drama at the surgery?'

It sounded like a *non sequitur*, but Juliet could see from his manner that it was not, so she answered seriously after some thought, 'Well, the mistake over the phone call is just something that can happen when a couple is flustered about the onset of labour. And fortunately it was such an easy delivery and such a healthy baby. . . But our set-up isn't geared for birth like a birthing centre, or even like a properly planned home delivery. It's a pity they were so convinced that they had to come to the surgery first.'

'Exactly!' he came in. 'But Vern insists that everyone do it, and there are times, like tonight, when it's simply not appropriate. He prides himself on predicting the course of labour accurately, and he *is* very good. If he tells a woman to go home because she won't be in active labour for another six hours, he's usually right, but "usually" isn't quite good enough for me.'

'It's not the only disagreement you have with Dr Gordon, is it?' she probed gently, remembering that she had seen signs of professional difference of opinion as early as last August.

'It's not even so much that we disagree. All doctors do that. No two practitioners think alike about everything, but I thought our different methods would create healthy debate and keep us on our professional toes.' He picked absently at the tangy and beautifully arranged platter of antipasto which, along with the deliciously dry Chablis, had been set down in front of them several minutes ago. 'It's the fact that he doesn't seem open to debate about it. It's not the impression I had of him when I agreed to join the practice, and Geoffrey, too, feels that Vern has changed lately.'

'Margaret and I were talking about it only today,' Juliet said slowly. 'She wants to find a way to suggest that he gets a full medical check-up.'

'Oh, lord! I'd better ring her on the weekend and tell her not to,' he sighed wearily.

'You made the same suggestion?'

'Yes.'

'And got short shrift?'

'In a way, but only because he'd *had* a check-up a week before I suggested it.'

'And the result?'

'A clean bill of health. But there *is* something he's not telling us. If you and Juliet have both noticed it too. . .'

'He went home early today. That's why you had to see Mrs Porter.'

'Yes, and according to Geoffrey that's fairly new, too. He always used to be the last to leave.'

'Could it be something. . .? His wife. Could there be a problem there?'

'Helen? Divorce? No, those two are——'

'I wasn't thinking of divorce,' she cut in, 'but of *Helen's* health.'

There was a pause and his narrowed hazel eyes met hers thoughtfully, then opened to reveal their full, sensitive depths. 'Juliet, you may have the answer. If Helen was ill, his mind would be miles away and of course he'd be impatient about long philosophical discussions on the finer aspects of pre-natal care.'

'And. . .I don't know him as well as you do, but isn't

he kind of man who would say nothing about it? If she had heart trouble, or. . .'

'Or cancer? Lord, yes! He'd tie himself in knots of guilt and blame for not having diagnosed it himself.'

'We're just guessing. . .'

'Yes. We are. But it adds up. I must find a way to get at the answer.'

'But if he wants it to be private. . .'

'Juliet, the way things have been going lately, it's jeopardising the practice. Something has to be said before. . .well, before I start looking for another partnership. I had an offer from a very good place in Sydney the other day.'

'Congratulations,' Juliet said automatically, only just managing to swallow the marinated artichoke heart she had forked into her mouth as he spoke.

'Hey! I'm not going yet!' he said lightly. 'In fact, I don't want to go at all. I've already said no to the Sydney people.'

Juliet's heart descended from her throat and settled back into its proper position, but her appetite seemed to have departed for good. Certainly the antipasto no longer held any appeal. The idea that Hugh might be leaving appalled her, and what appalled her even more was the effect that his words had had on her.

I thought I was over this, she thought to herself miserably. But I'm not over it at all!'

She tried to remember how she had recovered from her broken engagement to David and realised at once that the two things could not be related. So much less mature nine years ago, she had never felt this way about Hugh Beckhill's cousin.

'The Barossa Valley suits me,' he was saying now.

'In spite of the cumbersome Beckhill connection?' she probed lightly, taking a grip on her emotions.

'It's not always cumbersome. Uncle Lloyd is finally starting to accept that I'm a doctor, not a floating employee who can take on all the family's odd jobs. My father was happy with that—still is, running the office in Adelaide and travelling interstate regularly, but me? No!'

'No, it doesn't seem like your style,' Juliet murmured, thinking that she was learning a lot about Hugh tonight.

He interrupted the train of thought to say self-mockingly, 'Thank you for putting up with me tonight, Sister Rohan. This'll go down as double time on your wages.'

'Nonsense!'

'None the less, it's time we talked about something else.'

And, apparently without effort, he did find subjects to amuse and entertain her, and listened with lively, interested face to her own comments and anecdotes. Scarcely noticing that her appetite had returned and that the quiet restaurant had now filled with convivial Friday night groups, Juliet ate the aromatic pasta and pesto dish as well as the veal with its richly creamy sauce, and would have found room for dessert if Hugh had suggested it.

He didn't, though. 'This has been good, Juliet,' he said, leaning towards her, after their plates had been cleared away. 'Our talk about Vern was important, I think.'

'Yes,' she nodded. Important, but was it the only thing about the evening that had been good? She was deeply aware of him—of the light that shone on his dark hair, the pleasant aura of clean maleness that hovered around him, the two fine lines that grooved from his nose to the corners of his lips and hinted at the sensitivity she knew lay within him. With a sudden longing to trace those lines, to trace every detail of his face with tingling fingertips, she went on quickly, 'We needed the perspective of being away from the surgery to talk it through thoroughly.'

'The perspective of being away from the surgery,' he echoed thoughtfully, scarcely seemingly to look at her at all. 'Yes, there's a lot to be said for that. Perhaps we need to find that perspective more often.'

Five minutes later, they were out in the chilly night, surveying it from the shelter of the restaurant's small veranda.

'Brr!' He buttoned up his slate-grey coat, shaking his powerful shoulders. 'Unseasonably warm last week, and unseasonably cold tonight. Raining now, too. How about you? Ah, yes, good! You've got your jacket. Let's make a dash for it.'

And they did so—he to his vehicle and she to hers, so that there was only time for one brief, 'Goodnight,' called over the sound of the rain drumming on their car roofs, before they were each cocooned in a vehicle alone.

He flashed his lights at her before turning off on the road to Lyndhurst, where he lived in a bluestone house that was a larger version of her own cottage, and it was only then that she fully realised how much she had enjoyed being with him, and what hopes she had foolishly allowed to flourish within her. He had talked intimately to her tonight, but clearly the lessening of the distance that had existed over the past months between them meant nothing more than friendship. She had been a naïve, romantic fool to imagine it could be anything else.

CHAPTER NINE

'THIS is Juliet, everyone,' Chris Taylor said, ushering her into a rather crowded room and presenting her with a general flourish to the gathering, whose faces were largely a blur to Juliet.

It was never easy to meet a new collection of people who already knew each other, and she felt a little over-dressed in her grey suede trousers and white knitted top. Most of the men wore jeans or very casual trousers, while the women wore simple skirts or trousers.

She said a nervous, 'Hello,' but relaxed as Chris pointed out, 'You know several faces already from the hiking club. See, there's Paul, who's organising this, and his wife Sandy.'

'Yes. . . Hi, Paul. Hello, Sandy,' she said to the bearded high-school teacher and his freckled blonde wife. 'You've made this look very professional.'

She indicated the long table in front of them. It was covered with a crisp white damask cloth and stacked with dozens of tiny glasses and a crowd of filled and uncorked wine bottles.

'Yes, we wanted to do it properly,' Sandy said. 'I mean, why call it a wine-tasting if you're just going to serve it up as you normally do?'

'We're going to tell you about each wine—we'll start with the light things and move on to the heavy reds, of course—then pour a small taste, and people can make comments,' Paul explained. 'Then we'll take fresh glasses and go on to the next one.'

'You don't mean we'll have to all spit it into a swill barrel, do you?' a pretty honey-haired woman said with a moue of distaste.

'Well, Mary, yes, that *was* the plan,' Paul answered, deadpan.

'Oh, *yuck!*'

'But we couldn't get the barrel through the front door.'

Everyone laughed and Mary made a face. 'Oh, honestly! But how was I to know? I mean, people *do* do that at proper wine tastings. I've seen it on television.'

'And after the tasting we'll each choose which we liked best and have a decent glass of it to go with the fondue,' Paul finished.

His wife added, 'Meanwhile, there are lots of hors-d'oeuvres and some palate cleansers such as carrot sticks. Please help yourselves whenever you like as we go.'

The wine-tasting was fun. Having spent time with the Beckhill family, in which the subject of wine was inevitably serious business, Juliet enjoyed this irreverent attempt at connoisseurship. Paul talked very knowledgeably about each vintage, and only when they reached the eighth bottle did he admit that he'd rehearsed it all from the different wineries' own publicity material, or from newspaper articles and reviews he had been collecting since the beginning of the year.

Some people made earnest comments like, 'A very aromatic nose,' or, 'I like the spice notes,' or, 'A strong fruity aftertaste,' while others parodied the whole thing with, 'After*burn*, you mean,' and, 'The perfect adjunct to battered fish fingers and fried potato scallops.'

The half-filled thimble-size glasses, hired by the dozen from a catering firm, meant that Juliet had no trouble keeping up with the procession of different tastes, and was quite ready to try the tenth of Paul's planned dozen bottles.

'Now this,' he said, 'is my personal favourite. A Beckhill Cabernet Merlot, 1986, winner of the Gold Medal in its class in Paris, Melbourne and San Francisco, and described by Peter Mayhew in the *Herald* as. . .'

But Juliet had stopped listening at this point, scolding herself inwardly because even the anonymous presence of this wine made her think of Hugh. She was returned abruptly to the present when she felt Chris's arm land heavily on her shoulder, pulling her close to him so that they bumped rather roughly together.

'We have a personal connection with the Beckhill family here tonight,' he announced, clearly pleased at being able to create a stir of interest. 'Juliet works for one of them.'

'A spy! She'll probably go back and report what we said about all the rival wines!' said one of the most earnest tasters, his tone giving the words an aura of scandal.

'You work for them?' Paul looked put out, as if she had stolen his thunder somehow, or spoiled his carefully planned evening.

She said hastily, 'I'm a nurse. Hugh Beckhill is a doctor, an obstetrician and gynaecologist. He has almost nothing to do with the winery business.'

She had expected this explanation to defuse their interest, but unfortunately it didn't.

'Hugh Beckhill? I haven't heard of him,' one woman said. 'I've heard of Lloyd, that's the owner, and his son David who's training to take over. There was an article in *New Living* magazine last week about Beckhill House and its décor. His wife is pregnant and they're using Roslyn Tander, the interior designer, to do a nursery for the baby, et cetera, et cetera.'

'So how does this Hugh fit in, Juliet? Tell us some gossip!'

'He's David Beckhill's cousin,' she said, suppressing a sigh. 'And I'm afraid there isn't any gossip.'

'Oh, come on, there must be! Secret love-affairs, dynastic rivalry. . . Isn't your doctor bitter and jealous of David because he's going to inherit?'

'Yes, tell us what they're like!' Mary put in. 'Have you been to the house?'

'It looked fabulous in the magazine.'

'It does seem weird that your Dr Beckhill didn't go into the business.'

'Actually,' Juliet came in desperately, 'they're all quite ordinary and very nice. Hugh very much wanted to be a doctor, and——'

'Nice?' Paul said, with a slight sneer. 'No one who has that much money can be *nice*!'

'Are they really all that rich?' Mary wanted to know.

'Well, think about it!' Paul said jeeringly. 'It must be just about the biggest winery in the country. They have huge vineyards here in the Barossa Valley and all over the place. Every little old lady from Cairns to Perth drinks Beckhill's cream sherry, and the company has been around since about 1845. Come on, Juliet, if you're afraid it's going to get back to your boss, don't worry.'

'Hey, you're all embarrassing her!' Chris Taylor came in, his arm once again around Juliet's shoulders, this time protectively.

After a couple more comments, the subject was dropped, and she was grateful to Chris for stepping in. She sensed, though, at the same time, that he had enjoyed having her in the spotlight and using her to create a sensation, so her gratitude was mixed with irritation.

Chris was very nice—intelligent, rather quiet and serious, good-lookng in an outdoorsy sort of way with that beard and those woodsy-brown eyes. And he didn't know that she had good reasons for feeling sensitive about the subject of the Beckhill family, so her annoyance was probably unfair.

The rest of the evening was definitely spoiled, though. Several people, glancing rather apologetically in her direction, chose the Beckhill Cabernet Merlot as their favourite. Others, equally apologetically, chose one of the other wines, as did Juliet.

After the fondues, of which there were three, flavoured differently, the reader of *New Living* magazine, whose name turned out to be Gillian, came up to Juliet. 'I didn't choose the Beckhill wine just because I thought you'd report back,' she explained earnestly.

'I didn't think——' Juliet began.

'But have you really been to the house? What's it like? As gorgeous as it looked in the article?'

'It's very beautifully and tastefully done, yes, and so are the grounds.'

'Yes, I sneaked a look at those last summer when Adam and I——' she gestured at her tall, blond boyfriend '—went there for some cellar door tasting.'

In short, everyone treated her differently now, highlighting the fact, too, that she had dressed more elaborately than most people, and she wondered if giving them some of the 'gossip' they had asked for would have made things less awkward. She knew that by being reticent about the family she was seen as allying herself with them and became a snob in some people's eyes. In spite of the delicious fondues and some enjoyable snatches of talk with Chris and his friends, she wasn't sorry when the evening was over.

'There's something I've been wanting to tell you,' Chris said, as soon as they were settled in his somewhat elderly Range Rover ready for the drive home.

'Yes?'

'No, my timing's off. Let's wait till we get to your place.'

He talked about other things during the fifteen-minute drive—mainly his work as a geologist and how important it was to him, and how he wanted a personal life as well but wasn't sure how to order his priorities. There was an undercurrent of significance to what he said, and she suspected that all this was actually a precursor to something else.

'You see,' he said, switching off engine and headlights as he pulled on to the lush autumn grass in front of her cottage, so that they sat in the vehicle in darkness, 'I've just been given a job in Antarctica for a year. Found out yesterday afternoon. Another bloke was supposed to go but he can't make it, so they're sending me at very short notice. I have to leave next week before the weather fully closes in down there.'

She looked across at him, not knowing what to say, and unable to read the expression in his brown eyes. 'That's an important step in your career, isn't it?'

'Yes, a stint in Antarctica looks good on anyone's curriculum vitae. That's why I didn't hesitate about accepting it. But it means an end to our relationship, for the time being at least.'

'I understand.'

'Do you?' he asked eagerly. 'We can write, of course. Please *do* write,' he added carefully, as if afraid that he might have been too enthusiastic. 'I'll probably need letters from the outside world.'

'Of course I'll write.'

'A lot can happen in a year,' he said. 'So that's all I'll ask for. . .except this.'

She felt the padded seat move and creak as he bent towards her, his fingers reaching to the back of her neck to pull her face close to his. Their kiss was clumsy and uncertain, and although she had no active desire to fight free of his embrace she wasn't sorry when it ended.

He must have sensed her ambivalence. 'You're lovely,' he said. 'I wish. . . No, never mind. That's enough. Let's just say goodbye.'

'Goodbye, Chris. Thank you for tonight. I've enjoyed it, and our. . .' she hesitated, then chose the word '. . .friendship.'

And when she walked up the path, waved to him at the door as he turned the vehicle, and let herself into the small, cosy cottage, she knew that she felt no real loss at his departure from her life.

'There's bad news, Juliet,' Hugh said on Monday morning.

He had been the first to arrive at the surgery, and had opened everything up and switched on lights and heating as it was again a grey, cold and wet day. He had made coffee, too, and handed her a cup made just as she liked it, moderately strong with a generous splash of milk. Without taking a sip, she waited, feeling the heat of the thick china pressing into her palms as she gripped the mug in both hands.

'Helen Gordon *is* ill. A heart problem. She was admitted to hospital yesterday.'

'Oh, no!' Juliet whispered. 'So we were right. But there's no comfort in that.'

'None at all,' Hugh agreed. 'Vern and I had a good

talk together yesterday afternoon. Helen had a mild attack last August and they've been working on the condition since, with medication, diet and a very quiet life, but it wasn't enough.'

'Last August, and he never said a thing.'

'No. I asked him why and he said. . .well, there were lots of reasons, all of them very much Vern. Primarily, he thought it would affect the working of the practice.'

'Which it did anyway.'

'I know. I didn't say that, but he said it for me. He said he realised he had been moody and inflexible lately, not ready to try anything new in case it added to his workload.'

'And what's going to happen now?'

'He's taking today off.'

'*Today*? That's all?'

But Debbie and Margaret both arrived at that moment and had to be filled in on the news. Geoffrey, whom Dr Gordon had also spoken to yesterday, was still at the hospital following an early-morning delivery. Their first patients were due at any minute so little more could be said, but Hugh told them the most important news: Dr Gordon had decided to retire from practice.

Helen Gordon's illness and the uncertain future of Gordon and Associates cast a difficult atmosphere over the week. Julit visited the senior obstetrician's wife on Tuesday evening after work and found her cheerful and resilient, full of plans for her retirement to the coastal town of Robe which Juliet knew were too ambitious for someone with her heart problem.

Dr Gordon had outlined a different set of plans to them over lunch that day—first, a relaxing cruise, then selling the beach house at Robe and choosing something at Victor Harbour instead, as it was closer to the

Gordons' three children and to Adelaide's medical facilities, and better provided with low-key recreational activities. Juliet wondered how long it would take before Helen learned to live with her restricted future, and how she felt about her husband giving up his beloved medical work for her sake.

It isn't going to be easy for either of them, she thought.

The future of the practice was a different issue altogether. The three doctors snatched several meetings together during the week, closeted in Dr Gordon's office, and the three women began to wonder if they would find themselves without jobs by the end of the month.

'I wouldn't be surprised if Geoffrey went overseas,' Margaret speculated on Wednesday afternoon while she and Juliet were in the testing-room together. 'And that might be what Hugh will choose as well. Scotland or America for a couple of years, then heading a practice in his own name.'

'Then you don't think they'll buy Dr Gordon out?' Juliet said, the glucose-tolerance test she was working on suddenly held lifelessly in her hands. 'This beautiful building. . .'

'I know, and the good reputation they have from here to Salisbury, their popularity with the staff and management at the hospital. . . I'm just guessing, Juliet. There's no reason why things shouldn't continue smoothly, but my experience has been that once there is a jolt like this everything is called into question and people make quite unexpected choices.'

She was probably right, Juliet decided, remembering the way her own decision to come here had happened. Dr Gordon began scaling down his workload immediately, and by the end of the month, when Helen would still be in hospital, he planned to have made his last delivery. Then a locum would step in. 'Which is really just a procrastination until we reach a more definite decision,' Hugh said to Juliet late on Thursday afternoon.

'Do you have a preference?' she asked. 'As to the future, I mean.'

'I want to stay on here,' he said, 'but Vern's departure has made me feel restless. A stint elsewhere, if Geoffrey and I could arrange it so that I could come back in two or three years, is appealing at the moment.'

'Yes, Margaret thought you might want to try Scotland or America.'

'Did she?' he queried, with an enigmatic expression, then added suddenly, 'Alicia and David are having a barbecue on Sunday and they suggested I ask you. Would you like to come?'

'S-Sunday?' she stammered absurdly, playing for time. 'Let me think. I have friends coming up on Saturday, but Sunday is free. It sounds nice,' she ended lamely.

'I'll pick you up at noon, then, and I promise this event is neither formal nor enormous, so come casual and relaxed.'

'I will.' It was the first time he had referred to last spring's disastrous wine launch, and it was part of a softening she had noticed lately. They were both feeling more relaxed with each other, somehow.

If only I didn't have to spoil it by hoping for something more, she thought, remembering last Friday's dinner.

On Sunday morning, therefore, she schooled herself resolutely to appear, and be, simply friendly. It was a glorious day. The rain had eased at last yesterday morning, after over a week in which all the wheat and sheep farmers had been made so happy that the rest of the population could hope for sunshine without a guilty conscience. It was pleasantly mild, too, and the tang of autumn chill that clothed the air this morning should be gone by noon.

Juliet took Hugh at his word and wore casual stream-lined jeans and a patterned blouse in warm autumn tones, low-heeled shoes in natural leather and hair clipped back in a high pony-tail that emphasised the smooth shape of her head. She brought large-lensed sunglasses and a natural straw sun visor in case of sun and glare, and a light wool sweater in case of a cool breeze.

He called for her promptly at noon, dressed as casually as she was, in stone-white denim trousers and an open-necked blue and grey shirt that revealed a disturbing amount of the strong wall of his chest. Pushing this awareness firmly aside, she smiled at him and he grinned easily back. 'Perfect day for it, isn't it?' he said.

'Gorgeous.'

And they drove with a fresh breeze blowing through the Jaguar's open windows on the traffic-free roads.

'We're too early,' Hugh said, when they found that they were the only car parked in the wide curve of gravel.

'Yes, it really is quite a short trip cutting through the back roads and avoiding Romneyvale.'

They left the parking area and Hugh led the way along a stone-flagged walkway that rounded the side of the house and brought them to a patio, half-enclosed by shrubbery and also paved in stone. A barbecue grill was already set up there, its coals already glowing, and in the shade of the house stood two tables, one set with cold drinks and the other with mouth-watering salads

as well as all the traditional accompaniments to a
barbecue. Outdoor chairs were arranged in loose clus-
ters and some smaller round tables had large, colourful
umbrellas over them. There was no one else in sight,
however.

'Hmm. . .' Hugh said.

'I hope nothing's wrong,' Juliet put in.

'No, I think we're just early.' He looked up at a row
of windows on the second floor, and Juliet followed his
gaze. She saw David there, and he opened a window
and leaned out. 'We'll be down in a minute,' he called
cheerfully. 'Go for a walk, or you'll get stuck pouring
drinks for everyone else. I can see another car just
turning into the driveway.'

'We'll make our escape right now, then,' Hugh called
back, and he turned at once and grabbed Juliet's hand
to pull her through a narrow gap in the shrubbery that
led to a winding mossy path through the most private
part of the extensive grounds. 'Come on,' he said. 'I'd
like to be out of earshot of the new arrivals, or I'll feel
guilty about not deputising for David.'

Juliet laughed and quickened her pace, and soon
they were quite a distance from the house, approaching
the winery buildings themselves, through an avenue of
trees and beds of autumn chrysanthemums, with stands
of Australian native shrubs and flowers in the background, their reds and yellows vivid and their greens
subtle and muted.

'They must have an army of gardeners,' Juliet said.
'I knew it was beautiful, but not that it was as lovely as
this.'

'They have two or three,' Hugh said. 'Since the
public tours the winery and comes to the tasting room,
the place needs to look prosperous and confident in

itself. Visitors enjoy the wines more when they taste them in these circumstances.'

'That sounded very business-minded. You're more of a Beckhill than you realise, you know, Hugh!'

'Oh, I realise it,' he smiled. 'After all, we've been in the business for nearly a hundred and fifty years. That's partly why I'm thinking of going away for two or three years. To change the balance a little. As long as I can come back. Hang on,' he added. 'We're about to run into the cellar door car park, which would rather defeat the purpose of this expedition. Let's head back and take up our role as guests.'

But before they could turn back along the path, Juliet saw a blonde woman in large sunglasses and very figure-hugging white trousers turn away from a low reds sports car at the sound of Hugh's voice, and a second later she had started to walk rapidly towards them.

'Hugh!' she called, and he stopped.

'Anna! Hello!'

'Then we have come to the right place,' she said. 'I was just telling Anders that this was not right.' She spoke with a slight Scandinavian accent and the tall blond man who came up beside her at that moment looked so much like her that they had to be brother and sister. Juliet recognised something else, too. This was the woman whose voice she had heard on the phone at the surgery more than once lately, asking to speak to Hugh.

'No, you *have* come the wrong way,' he answered. 'This is just the public entrance to the winery and the cellar door tasting room. To get to the private driveway to the house you need to. . .' He stopped, then went on. 'Unfortunately it's difficult to explain. Much easier if we jump in the car and come with you. We were just heading back there anyway.'

Anders and Anna exchanged a glance and Anders asked a question in Swedish which drew a long and energetic reply. It was evident that he didn't speak much English, and Anna was explaining to him what was going on. At the end of it, she turned back to Hugh and Juliet, saying, 'But our car we have hired is only a two-seater. Anders likes sports cars,' she explained casually. 'Could you come with me, Hugh, and your friend. . .?'

'I'm sorry,' he came in quickly. 'I've been very rude, not introducing you. This is Juliet, who works with us in the practice. Juliet, Anna and Anders are about to start a wine-importing business at home in Stockholm, and they're on an extensive world tour at the moment, researching the wines they want to sell. Can I send you back with Anders, while I show Anna in the car?'

'Of course,' she nodded politely, not quite knowing what to think. 'Anders, come with me. It's a beautiful walk through the gardens.'

He nodded and said, 'Walk? I like,' and they started off.

Behind her, Juliet heard the red sports car roar impatiently into life and was aware of its arrogant buzz coming and going at intervals throughout the walk, as it took the indirect route by road to the house's pillared entrance gate. Anders was a silent companion, and after eliciting from him through a series of awkward phrases that he was indeed Anna's brother, and her twin at that, she allowed silence to fall between them, thinking that all she needed now was to get lost on these pathways and the awkwardness of the encounter with the two Swedes would be complete.

But they arrived at the sandstone patio uneventfully,

to find David and Alicia ensconced as hosts and about a dozen people gathered and already enjoying drinks and nuts as lamb chops, sausages and Indonesian satays sizzled appetisingly on the grill. Anna and Hugh arrived a few minutes later, and Juliet couldn't help wondering if it really had taken them that long to make the drive.

If he is involved with her, though, what difference does it make? she asked herself, determined to keep the happy equilibrium with which she had begun the day. They have a perfect right to be happy together and I wish them luck.

Shaking off her awareness of the couple, she went up to Alicia and David, who were both at work around the barbecue grill, and both looked happy and relaxed together. David greeted her easily, as if it were only a week since they had seen each other.

'It's getting close now,' Alicia said, touching her growing stomach. She was neatly and prettily dressed today in blue denim maternity overalls with a floral blouse beneath. 'Our childbirth class starts in about four weeks. Will you be running it?'

'I'm not sure yet,' Juliet answered. 'Margaret and I take it in turns, or if there's a big group we do it together. We haven't got all the enrolments in yet.'

'I sent mine in a month ago.'

'I know, but you're one of our eager beavers. It'd be easier to plan ahead if we had more of them!' She didn't mention the greater uncertainty that hung over all the practice's future plans at the moment.

The next two hours passed in eating and talking, and Juliet chatted to Anne Thomas and her husband about their restaurant business, and heard about the new developments in their four-month-old baby girl, who was asleep upstairs in a spare room, monitored by the baby intercom that Anne kept carefully beside her.

As well, she made the effort to talk to Anders again, since, when he was not beside his sister who could interpret for him, his poor command of English meant that he was rather left out. She was nodding in encouragement as Anders attempted laboriously to explain how long they had been in Australia and how long they planned to remain, when Hugh caught her eye across the gathering and came over, with Anna still smiling with very white teeth at his side.

'Anna and Anders, will you excuse Juliet and myself for a while?' he said to the blond Swedes. 'We have some business to discuss.'

'Of course,' Anna said prettily, and immediately turned to Anders, who launched a long monologue of Swedish at her.

Hugh took Juliet's arm and steered her to the fringe of the gathering, collecting strawberry pavlova for each of them while Juliet took two coffees from the steaming tray that had just been brought out. They sat side by side in low white wooden chairs, placing the desserts on the small table in between, and she turned to him questioningly. Had he been called into the house for a medical phone call when she hadn't noticed?

'I'm sorry about Anna,' he said, and for one awful moment she thought he had noticed her painful awareness of the time he was spending with the blonde Swede.

'Please don't apologise for a friendship, Hugh,' she began, her cheeks growing hot at once.

'Friendship?' he gave a bark of laughter. 'To be honest, she's becoming very much of a chore.'

'A *chore*?'

'Don't ask me to go into detail about how I fend her

off on the personal level, but in business terms I can't afford to alienate her. The Lauerson twins have a lot of money to spend.'

'Yes, they certainly give that impression,' Juliet agreed, her heart ridiculously light at the realisation that Hugh wasn't involved with Anna at all. She couldn't meet Hugh's gaze, and stared down at her dessert as if it was the most interesting thing she had ever seen. 'Anders said they've been here a month already, and, if I understood him properly, the whole trip is open-ended, with plans to go to America and most of the wine-producing countries of Europe as well.'

'Apparently, yes. We were a bit suspicious at first, their plans were so hazy. We thought they might be planning some sort of scam, but no, they're quite genuine. They came into a large inheritance and decided to go into the wine-importing field, but they're in no hurry to actually start on the hard work. Clearly they will eventually, so we need to do what we can to make them order large consignments of Beckhill wines, but I must say, I'm more than ready for them to do an in-depth study of the Hunter Valley wine-growing region, nine hundred miles away in New South Wales!'

They laughed and began their dessert and coffee, and when his hazel eyes met her own blue ones she almost thought for a moment that the fire of awareness that had been so strong between them last August had returned. But it disappeared as quickly as it had come and seconds later she doubted whether she had seen it at all.

Shortly after this, the gathering began to break up, and Juliet found herself at Hugh's side in the dark green Jaguar, heading for home. The sun flashed through the trees as they drove and she felt pleasantly sleepy after the lengthy meal in the middle of the day. For a few minutes they chatted casually as friends would, then silence fell between them, and that felt nice and friendly, too.

Perhaps I *am* going to be able to do this after all, she thought drowsily. . .

She was awoken five minutes later by a warm hand cupping her shoulder gently. 'Home, Juliet. . .'

She stirred into wakefulness, a little embarrassed, and felt his warm breath against her cheek like a caress as he leaned towards her from the driver's seat. As her eyes opened fully, they met his, and she saw the twinkle of a smile there.

'I should have let you sleep,' he said.

'You could hardly do that!'

'Perhaps not.'

'This has been lovely, Hugh.'

'I'll pass on your thanks to Alicia and David.'

'I thanked them already, but yes, when you see them again do tell them what a perfect afternoon it was.'

'I will.'

'Goodbye, then.' She climbed out of the car, wanting to ask him in, to prolong their time together, but he had remained comfortably in the driver's seat and the engine of the vehicle still purred. Sensibly, she decided to end the afternoon on a high note of warmth and not look for more than the simple friendship he seemed to be offering now.

'Bye, Juliet,' he said. 'See you on Monday.'

And by the time she had walked up the path to her front door the Jaguar was gone.

CHAPTER TEN

'ALL right, next revision question,' Margaret said. 'Again, this is just for husbands, otherwise the wives answer all the time, I've found,' she added rather sternly, and a couple of the men, who hadn't shown themselves very familiar with what they had been taught in the childbirth classes, looked sheepish. 'When should your wife begin her special breathing? David?'

'When she can no longer sit, talk or walk through a contraction,' David Beckhill answered promptly, and Alicia patted his knee fondly, pleased that he was so well-prepared.

Juliet noticed the gesture, and his answering smile, and felt very happy for them. Looking at David these days she almost never thought of him as the man she had once been engaged to. His relationship with Alicia had become so much stronger in the course of her pregnancy, it seemed, and his character seemed to have strengthened, too, with the success of the white Zinfandel wine he had introduced. It was already the second biggest seller of the Beckhill wines, Hugh had mentioned recently, and had a high profile with the general public through its successful advertising and promotion, largely master-minded by David himself. The imperious and too-arrogant Lloyd had had to recognise that his son was no longer a mere trainee and was ready to take over the full reins of the family company.

'It gives me peace of mind,' Hugh had said recently, during the kind of friendly talk that was becoming more frequent between him and Juliet. 'This time last year, I was seriously worried that he might be heading for a breakdown, and the strain on Alicia was showing badly. It was one of the reasons I was keen to accept the partnership here, to be closer to both of them. Now I can go off to Scotland in September with nothing to worry about.'

Because his stint overseas was soon to become a reality. In the seven weeks since the barbecue at the Beckhill estate, the future of the obstetrics and gynaecology partnership had been finalised. Dr Gordon had sat in on the process of choosing a new third partner, and a dynamic thirty-five-year-old New Zealander, Fred Amey, had been offered the opportunity. He was back in Wellington now, with his wife and child, packing their belongings ready for the big move, and would be starting next week. The locum they had now would remain in a floating role until September, when he would fill Hugh's three-year vacancy.

Helen Gordon was out of hospital and starting to regain some fitness, although she had been told to lead a very easy life. Vern had taken on the extra burden of care devotedly, and came to the practice now only when needed for special consultation.

Change was in the air, and not least for the eleven couples in this month's class. Alicia Beckhill's due date was now less than three weeks away. In some ways, her pregnancy seemed to Juliet to have gone frighteningly fast, while in other ways so much had happened since she had come to the Barossa Valley last year that it seemed half a lifetime ago.

After the review session ended, there was a final fifteen minutes of open questioning and discussion which broke down into happy general chatter, then the class ended in general hilarity as three of the husbands, one of whom was David, organised a sweep to predict which of their babies would come first, as all three of their wives were due on the fifteenth of June.

'I know it won't be me,' Alicia groaned, getting heavily to her feet. She had put on twelve kilograms, which looked as if it was all baby, and was starting to find day-to-day activity difficult. 'I'll still be waddling around clutching my lower back when you two are home putting alphabet friezes around the nursery walls!' she said to the other two women.

As it turned out, though, she *was* the first to go, labour beginning in the early hours of the morning on the twelfth of June. Hugh came in to the surgery that morning with the news, having stopped at the hospital on the way in to examine her.

'Only two centimetres dilated,' he reported. 'It'll probably be a while before anything happens, although her contractions are nice and close together. I've told her and David to try and walk around if they can for the next couple of hours, to try and bring the baby lower and strengthen the contractions. Her waters haven't broken yet.'

Nothing was heard from the hospital for the rest of the day, and by the time they were ready to close the surgery for the day Juliet sensed his mounting tension.

'No news yet?' she asked.

'No.' He shrugged off her question impatiently, then added reluctantly, 'I called at two and she was up to five centimetres, but the contractions seemed to be slowing down. She had got too tired walking and wanted to rest.'

'Her waters?'

'Still haven't broken. Might have to do it myself to speed things up. I'm going to phone again now.'

'Still, for a first pregnancy. . .'

'No, nothing unusual about it. The head hadn't engaged last time I examined her, and that often slows things down. It's going to be a big baby, I think. . . Anyway, I'll ring now.'

He turned to the phone, the wall of his strong shoulders indicating dismissal and a desire to be alone. Juliet felt a twinge of anxiety as she left his office and gathered her things, although there was no reason to. As he had said, perhaps as much to reassure himself as for any other reason, this was quite a normally developing labour so far.

'No news?' Margaret repeated Juliet's own question to Hugh, and she relayed the report that he had just given to her. 'I've forgotten. When did her labour start?' Margaret asked.

'About two.'

'Mm, she'll be starting to tire.'

At that moment, Hugh catapulted from his office, his manner completely changed. 'Eight centimetres,' he shouted on the run. 'They were just picking up the phone to ring here when I got through. Waters broken, and going strong. See you tomorrow!' He dashed out to his car.

'That man!' Margaret shook her head ruefully, and Juliet turned to her fellow nurse, puzzled. She had just been thinking how deeply he cared about Alicia and how right he was in the profession he had chosen, but this sounded like a criticism coming.

'What do you mean?' she blurted.

Margaret sighed. 'He needs a wife,' she said simply, 'or he'll be half in love with his cousin's. And he needs a child or two not too far down the line. He'll make a gorgeous father. Perhaps we'll have to hope that he comes back in three years with a red-haired Scottish lassie. . .'

'Yes.'

'. . .although if it's redheads he wants we have a few good specimens of those much closer to home, don't we, Juliet?'

Juliet turned away with a non-committal response as a thick, glossy strand of her own copper-auburn locks fell against the curve of one hot cheek. Not for the first time, she was horribly afraid that Margaret had guessed her feelings for Hugh, and was scolding the obstetrician for not returning them. She wanted to say, 'Please don't try and fight my battles for me, Margaret,' but that would only give her secret away for certain. As for Margaret's theory that Hugh was hovering on the brink of love for Alicia, that had to be an exaggeration, didn't it?

A few minutes later, they locked the surgery and left.

Hugh telephoned two hours after Juliet arrived home. 'A boy,' he said. 'Michael Lloyd. Over eight pounds. We thought it would be quite large, and we were right. Mother and baby both doing well. Father over the moon. She had a hard time in second stage, pushed for an hour and a half.'

'Then you're still at the hospital?'

'Yes. I'm about to go home.'

She hesitated, wanting to say, Why not drop in for a bite to eat? You must be tired, but in the end she didn't, and came out with a simple, 'Thanks for letting me know, Hugh,' instead.

'I thought you'd want to hear. Whew! I'm relieved it's over.'

'There was no reason for fear, though, was there?'

'No, and after seeing hundreds of deliveries I should be immune to any kind of nerves, but somehow, when it's someone you know and care about. . .'

'You forget all the normal deliveries and conjure up the few that have gone wrong, in all their graphic detail,' Juliet finished for him.

'Exactly! And it would have broken them both if something *had* gone badly wrong, or if the baby hadn't been all right. They need the sun shining on them, those two. Some people. . .like you, I think. . .manage much better under adversity.'

She didn't know if it was a compliment. Perhaps it was simply an observation. She decided to take it that way and answered simply, 'Perhaps you're right.'

There was a tiny pause, then, 'I'd better go,' and the phone clicked and gave a low buzz almost before she had said goodbye.

Juliet went to visit Alicia two days later, dropping in at the labour ward on her way in, to say hello to the nurses. She spoke to them quite often by phone, but rarely got to see them face to face. Jenny Barnes was on duty and she spotted Juliet as soon as the latter entered.

'Come to check up on us?' she said, coming forward.

The place seemed busy tonight, with nearly all the labour-rooms occupied, although only one woman, in early labour, was a patient from the Romneyvale practice. Jenny and Juliet talked for a while, but then the other nurse was needed on the ward and Juliet made her way round to post-partum, with an inevitable stop at the nursery window.

Michael Lloyd Beckhill, just forty-eight hours old, was lined up in front along with several other babies, all wrapped like tight little bundles in pastel-patterned flannel blankets. He had a thicket of silky black hair all over his head, and a red face marked, as most newborns were, with bruises from his difficult passage through the birth canal.

He was asleep at the moment, his eyes tightly closed and his little fists seeming to struggle to break free of their swaddling. Juliet observed as much about the baby as she could, knowing that Alicia would think him the most beautiful creature in the world, and the most fascinating of all possible conversation topics.

She had found out Alicia's room number at the front desk downstairs, and since she knew her way around the maternity wing she was able to go there confidently, with a smile of greeting and congratulations ready on her lips for Alicia, and for David who would probably be there as well.

At first she thought it *was* David—the masculine figure clad in dark trousers and a grey and white shirt, bent over the raised upper half of the bed and holding Alicia in a long, close embrace. Then, as Alicia raised her face from his neck just enough to speak effusively into his ear, she saw that it wasn't David at all.

'Hugh, oh, *darling* Hugh!' Alicia whispered. 'I don't know what I'd do without you!' She pressed her face into his neck again, then turned it slightly so that her lips travelled over his cheek.

Soundlessly, heart pounding in her chest, Juliet turned on her heel and fled the room, a gasp of horror escaping her lips at the last moment. What had Margaret said only the other day? That Hugh was half in love with Alicia?

And I thought she was exaggerating! she thought in shock.

A deeper voice inside her whispered painfully that she had also been starting to cherish a foolish hope that Hugh's friendliness lately might develop into something more. Would she ever learn? Rounding the corner on her instinctive way to the lift, she almost careened into a group of five people and as masculine arms came out to steady her she heard David's voice near by.

'Juliet! Are you all right?'

'Yes, I. . .I just remembered I left something in the oven and forgot to switch it off,' she improvised at a gabble as she took in David's group.

It had been the formidable Lloyd's arms that had steadied her and he was frowning down at her now, clearly wondering what on earth she was doing here. Barbara Beckhill's greeting was polite but chilly, and then David introduced Alicia's parents. The whole group was obviously on its way to visit Alicia and the baby, and Juliet's instinct was only to protect them from the discovery of David's wife and his cousin in each other's arms.

'You're here to see Alicia? But you *must* see the baby first!' she gushed, in an effusive way that was completely unlike her. 'He's *divine*, the little darling. Alicia is so happy!'

'You've just seen her?'

'Er—yes, but only briefly. As I said. . .' She trailed off. Hugh had come up to the group, and as he greeted them she murmured quickly, 'The oven. . . My casserole. . .' and side-stepped away, seeing the green light come on above the lift and hearing its ping with a stab of painful relief.

Entering it and finding herself happily alone, she looked quickly for a 'Door Close' button but couldn't find one and fumbled for the ground-floor button instead, losing precious seconds. The door seemed to be taking forever to close, and then just as her fervent entreaties to it were at last being answered Hugh reached the lift and threw an arm out to press the closing doors back again.

'Hello,' she said inadequately as the lift travelled downwards, her face frozen in a mask of self-control.

'Juliet. . .'

'I have to run. I left something in the oven.' It was as good an excuse as any, and at least created a consistent story.

'Wait!'

'No!' The door opened and she spun out into the main foyer, crossing it at a furious clicking pace in her black leather court shoes.

'*Wait*, I said!'

They were outside the building now, passing by some shrubs that bordered the concrete path which led to the visitor's car park, and suddenly her anger exploded.

'You saw me there in the doorway, didn't you?' she demanded, stopping in her tracks and wheeling around to face him.

'Heard you, as you left,' he answered briefly, showing no guilt or shame.

'And you're going to "explain"?'

'Alicia is having——'

'I don't want to hear it! Why should I? What's sauce for the gander is sauce for the goose, isn't it?' she fumed. 'Last year you caught me in David's arms and it put an end to what was happening between us without me ever having a chance to tell you my side of the story. Now the boot is on the other foot. I see you in the arms of a married woman, and I'm expected to hear your rational explanation and understand. Well, I *don't* understand and I *won't*! I——'

'Juliet!' He was actually laughing, gripping her by the shoulders and laughing into her face as the evening breeze caught at his hair and tossed it over his high, smooth forehead. 'In the arms of a married woman?'

he echoed. 'Is that what you mind about? Were you jealous of Alicia because of *me*?'

Caught up in the tumult and release of her anger, even more furious because he seemed to be laughing at her, she was still too emotional to care what she was saying. 'Of course because of you! Who else? How could you possibly be blind enough to think that I still have an iota of feeling for *David* apart from the fact that he's *your* cousin! My goodness, it will be a relief when you go to Scotland and I can start getting you out of my system!'

Then suddenly he was very serious. 'Juliet, darling, please, *please*, don't get me out of your system! Please keep me right in there, the way I've got you in mine.'

'What? Am I expected to——?'

'I wasn't kissing Alicia. I was hugging her. There's a difference, you know. Look, I'll show you. A hug. . .' He cradled her against his shoulder and helplessly she felt the tide of her anger ebbing, leaving her breathless and tingling, exhilarated, horrified and wary, all at the same time. 'Now *this*, my darling, is a kiss. . .'

And there was no doubt about it, it was—a very thorough and expert kiss that coaxed a response from her before she knew whether she wanted to give one. It began gently and teasingly, but soon his lips had deepened their pressure on hers, parting them to find the sweetness within, and sending ripples of melting awareness to every nerve-ending. His hands moulded the curves of her hips, pulling her closer to him so that she felt the hardness of his thighs against hers, and if they hadn't been in a public place she knew that both of them would have found it hard to call a halt to what was happening.

'What were you saying about Alicia?' she asked

weakly when he finished what he had pretended was a mere demonstration.

'First, before we say anything else, Juliet,' he answered, 'let's get one thing straight. I love you.'

'Do you?'

'Yes, and I'm starting to realise that it's *not* going to go away! As to Alicia, she was having some post-partum blues. She had a tiring time and she didn't rest enough yesterday—too excited about the baby. Today, the hormones kicked in and she started worrying about the reality of a baby, and her skills as a mother. Very real feelings, but they'll pass in a day or two, I'm sure. She needed a shoulder to cry on, and since I care about her a lot, as David's wife and because she's a very nice person, I was happy to provide it.'

'And yet when David needed the same thing last year. . .'

'I thought all the wrong things, I wouldn't listen and I brought in far too many fears and doubts of my own. In short, I was an unforgivable idiot,' he came in freely. 'But we can't talk about it here. There's the doctors' lounge just in here. I only hope it's empty!'

He pulled her along with him through a side-entrance and down a corridor, and then they entered a modest-sized room strewn with comfortable chairs and coffee-tables, which was fortunately unoccupied at the moment, although an urn boiled on a bench-top where tea- and coffee-making facilities were stored.

'I was an idiot,' Hugh repeated, wasting no time. 'Or perhaps. . . I don't know. . . The fact that you'd once been involved with David was hard.'

He was pacing the room restlessly and Juliet stood transfixed in the middle, needing his touch. Finally, she went up to him. 'Hugh, if this is an important talk. . .'

He seemed to understand straight away. 'Do we need to be doing *this*?' he asked, enclosing her softly with his arms and gazing down at her.

'I—I think so.'

'Perhaps even this?' He bent towards her and her 'yes' was murmured against his lips as she felt the wall of his chest rise and fall with his breathing against the warmth of her own body. It was utterly reassuring, utterly sensual, and hearing the words he had used '. . .I love you. . .' over and over in her mind, she wondered for long minutes if any explanations were needed at all. Then she knew that, for both of them to feel fully free to be carried with this tide, they were.

'You see,' Hugh said, still holding her close, 'I've always felt like this about you, but when your engagement to David was broken—by you, as I thought at the time—I let you disappear out of loyalty to him. And, too, I wasn't ready. I know you weren't, and that you were barely aware of my existence. . .'

'I was a complete ninny in those days.'

'I forgot all about you until you turned up to work with us and from the very beginning we seemed to slip into place beside one another so naturally—at times. At other times, all I could see was how uncomfortable you still seemed about David, how unconvincing you were, even to yourself, when you insisted it was all resolved. And I could see that for David the thing had never been finished. I didn't trust my own ability to make you forget David and love me fully.'

'But no,' Juliet said. 'I think it *was* finished between David and me. If he and Alicia hadn't been having problems he never would have suggested otherwise and I would have been able to leave the whole thing in the past, where it belonged. But you're right. I was as wary and awkward as you. . .'

'And I was frightened by that, instead of realising it was just something you needed time to get through. We had that rift at the night of the wine launch, which at first I told myself was the only answer, but which I've regretted for a long time.'

'Why didn't you say anything?'

'I wasn't sure that you were still interested. You seemed to have your life well under control. Then lately I began to suspect that I did still have a chance. But we rushed it last time. This time I wanted to take things slowly. And I still wasn't sure. Lately, I've been trying to be a friend, not knowing if I'd ever be any more than that. . .'

'And planning to go to Scotland in three months' time. Was I supposed to find that encouraging?' she scolded.

He shrugged helplessly. 'Will you come with me?'

'To Scotland?'

'Of course. There's time to organise a wedding between now and then, isn't there?' he said against her lips.

'A *wedding*?'

'An early September wedding, with a honeymoon in Paris on the way to Edinburgh. Juliet, say you will. Say it's all right and that all this doubt about the past is behind us now!'

Her answer was not in words, but the gift of herself to him in the expression of her blue eyes and in the press of her body against his was clearer than any words could be, and very fortunately it was another fifteen minutes before two anaesthetists came in, in search of coffee.

'Don't mind us,' Hugh said happily. 'We were just leaving.'

And they went out arm in arm, oblivious to raised

eyebrows and speculative looks. 'Shall we go and tell Alicia and David our news?' he asked her.

And when she gave as her very decided answer, 'No, let's *not* bring them into it for at least a week!' David Beckhill's cousin threw back his head, lifted her and swung her around him giddily, and laughed.

DON'T MISS EUROMANCE

1992 is a special year for European unity, and we have chosen to celebrate this by featuring one Romance a month with a special European flavour.

Every month we'll take you on an exciting journey through the 12 countries of the European Community. In each story the hero will be a native of that country–imagine what it would be like to be kissed by a smouldering Italian, or wined and dined by a passionate Frenchman!

Our first **EUROMANCE**, *The Alpha Man'* by Kay Thorpe is set in Greece, the land of sunshine and mythology. As a special introductory offer we'll be giving away *'Hungarian Rhapsody'* by another top author, Jessica Steele, absolutely free with every purchase of *'The Alpha Man'*.

And there's more . . .

You can win a trip to Italy simply by entering our competition featured inside all Romances in September and October.

Published: September 1992   Price: £1.70

-MEDICAL ♥ ROMANCE-

The books for enjoyment this month are:

GYPSY SUMMER Laura MacDonald
THE BECKHILL TRADITION Lilian Darcy
THE DOCTORS AT SEFTONBRIDGE Janet Ferguson
A MIDWIFE'S CHOICE Margaret Holt

♥ ♥ ♥ ♥ ♥

Treats in store!

Watch next month for the following absorbing stories:

A PERFECT HERO Caroline Anderson
THE HEALING HEART Marion Lennox
DOCTOR'S TEMPTATION Sonia Deane
TOMORROW IS ANOTHER DAY Hazel Fisher